a Walk in the Sun

Also by
Michelle Zink

Lies I Told
Promises I Made

PROPHECY OF THE SISTERS TRILOGY
Prophecy of the Sisters
Guardian of the Gate
Circle of Fire

a Walk in the Sun

MICHELLE ZINK

HARPER TEEN
An Imprint of HarperCollinsPublishers

HarperTeen is an imprint of HarperCollins Publishers.

A Walk in the Sun
Copyright © 2016 by Michelle Zink
www.epicreads.com

ISBN 978-0-06-243446-3

Typography by Torborg Davern
16 17 18 19 20   CG/RRDH   10 9 8 7 6 5 4 3 2 1
❖
First Edition

For Alex Blazeski,
who lives on in the land he loved
and in the hearts of those who loved him

One

Rose Darrow groaned, reaching through the darkness to swipe the alarm on her phone. She didn't need to look to know that it was four a.m. She closed her eyes again, remembering how it used to be, the morning sun slanting softly into her bedroom on school days, the cows calling to her dad across the field out back while her mom banged around in the kitchen.

She forced her eyes open. Living in the past wouldn't get her through today.

She swung her legs over the side of the bed and shuffled to the bathroom, then pulled on her work jeans and a T-shirt. At least it was warmer now and slightly less depressing than the cold winter mornings right after her mother's funeral. Then it had seemed like the whole world had died, like her mom had taken the sun and the flowers and the smell of fresh-cut grass with her forever. Now the land was coming back to life even if her mom was gone for good. It was hard not to feel betrayed by the knowledge.

She braided her hair in the dark and stepped into the hallway, silent except for the grandfather clock ticking softly in the entryway downstairs. She held still, taking a few seconds to listen for her dad. She knew it was pointless, but she couldn't help herself, couldn't stop hoping that one day he would rise above his sadness and remember that Rose was still there. That she needed him.

Finally she gave up and padded quietly down the stairs. She pulled on her boots, her eyes on the picture of her mother that hung in the foyer. People had been telling Rose that she looked like her mother since she was old enough to walk. Same red hair, same green eyes, both of them a little on the tall side. She hadn't liked it when she was younger. She'd wanted to look like herself then. Like Rose, not Kate Darrow's daughter. But looking at the picture now, she hoped it was true, like their similarities might somehow prove that her mother had once really existed when her presence seemed more like a dream with each passing day.

Rose stared at the picture of her mother a few seconds longer. Then she headed for the barn.

Everything was still and quiet, the moon high in the velvety sky, as she made her way across the dirt road that separated the house from the cattle barn. At seventy-five acres, the farm was small by some standards, but it was a lot of land, all of it laid out around the house at its center. Rose felt overwhelmed just looking at it.

She should be relieved that Aunt Marty had hired someone to help over the summer. School would be out soon, giving Rose more hours to work on the farm, but it still wouldn't be enough. There were fences to mend and irrigation pipes to repair, vaccinations to give and numbers to calculate, the weight of the cattle and the amount of money they would bring always a precarious balance against the cost of grain. There was the garden to maintain and the market stand to run, more crucial than ever now that money was tight. And then there was the hay; the entire north pasture would have to be cut and baled. Will Breiner was a good friend, but he was busy on his own farm. She couldn't expect him to keep doing double duty, and there was no way Rose could do it alone.

Still, the farm was more than a business. It didn't matter that it had started to feel like an anchor around her feet; the rhythm of it was in her blood. It felt weird to think of a stranger living in the bunkhouse, working alongside her day in and day out. She hoped he knew what he was doing at least.

She headed for the heifers and their calves first. Seven babies had been born in February, and they hadn't lost a single one, something Rose was especially proud of since she'd taken charge of the whole thing. Will and his dad had helped a little, but most nights, it was Rose who stayed up waiting to make sure the mothers and their babies were okay. When the bedding was dirty and needed to be changed, she was the one who mucked the stalls before and after school. When one of her mother's heifers had had trouble giving birth, she'd texted Will and her aunt Marty, then got the calving chains, wrapping them around the calf's legs the way her dad had shown her last year and pulling gently when the cow had a contraction. It had taken her less than twenty minutes to birth the calf, a frail-looking female with fur the color of fresh hay. By the time Will and Aunt Marty got there, Rose was sitting on the floor, her chest feeling simultaneously full and empty as she watched the baby try to nurse.

She opened the door to the barn and was immediately greeted with the bawls of the mother cows. The calves wouldn't be weaned for months, but the mothers knew when they saw Rose that it meant feeding time. It hadn't always been that way. When her dad had first stopped coming to the barn, when he'd started sleeping odd hours and forgetting the chores, the cows had just looked at her, blinking, like they had no idea who she was or what she was doing there. It's not like she hadn't done her share before, but her dad had always been so enthusiastic about the farm that he'd taken care of almost everything himself, hiring local help for the busy seasons of hay and harvest and trading work on the Breiners' dairy farm for a hand with the bigger stuff. Rose had been in charge of feeding the chickens, harvesting food from the garden planted by her mom, sometimes bottle-feeding a clueless calf. It was her dad the cows turned to for food, and she used to laugh out loud when she'd see them running to him like excited kids from across one of the pastures.

Now they lined up at the trough as soon as they saw Rose, and she walked to the feed chute and turned the hand crank. A second later, the feed, earthy and sour, started to pour out of the chute. It funneled into the trough, unfurling out of the barn through a hole in the wall while the cows waited patiently, watching the grain make its way toward them.

When the trough was full all the way down the line, Rose stopped turning the crank. She opened the door between the pen and the interior of the barn and leaned against the doorjamb so she could watch them while they ate. The babies were still trying to suckle while their mothers ate breakfast. All except for Buttercup, the little female Rose had birthed. The calf stood off to the side, the green fly tag in her ear twitching as she watched the others eat.

She was still too small, and worry thrummed through Rose's mind when she thought of all the trouble they'd had with the calf. At first everything had seemed fine. She had suckled on her mother just like she was supposed to, ingesting the nutrient-rich milk that was essential to her newborn health. But she had never fed easily again, and Rose had spent the last four months trying everything to get the calf to eat regularly. Sometimes she'd walk in and be surprised to find the baby nursing, but it never lasted long, and her weight hadn't kept pace with the other babies' in the barn. Rose had even tried bottle-feeding the animal, but that hadn't worked, either, the calf pulling her head out of Rose's grasp, bawling and backing away even when she usually seemed happy to see Rose. Rose had spent so much time with her that she'd finally given her a name, though that was something they didn't usually do. All of the calves would eventually be sold to cattle farms, most of them out west. Giving them names was an easy way to make yourself miserable when you had to say goodbye.

But this one had come from a heifer with a green tag, the mark of her mother's hand in her breeding. Rose's mom had had an affinity for breeding, an instinct for which heifers and bulls to buy at auction and when to bring them together. The farm had been in her blood, too, and Rose had named the struggling calf after her mother's favorite flower. Right now, there were still a few other green-tagged calves, but they would all be sold in the fall, Buttercup included, and then there would never be another animal on the farm that had been bred by Rose's mother.

Resolving to talk to Will about the calf, Rose closed the door to the feed room and headed to the house. Careful not to wake her dad, she grabbed some cleaning supplies, a fresh set of sheets, some towels, and a broom, then made her way to the old bunk room at the back of the barn.

The room hadn't been used in decades as far as she knew, and she cringed as she opened the door, scared of what she would find. But it was just a dusty room with four bunks, two beds apiece, a dresser, and an old wooden dining table. The concrete floor was covered with dirt, and she went to work sweeping and dusting before moving on to the small bathroom. She left the sheets and towels on the dresser and opened the window to let in some fresh air. She might not be happy about the idea of a stranger on the farm, but she wouldn't be inhospitable. That was something her mother never would have tolerated.

When the room was as clean as could be expected, she left the big barn and headed for the smaller one where she spent the next hour feeding and watering the horses and mucking their stalls before moving on to the chickens.

The sky was just beginning to lighten when she headed to the house for a shower.

Two

It was mid-May when Bodhi Lowell finally reached New York. It had taken him almost two months of walking, two months with nothing but the pack on his back and his own thoughts for company, but he'd made it all the way from Montana, and for the first time in his whole life he found himself east of the Mississippi.

He'd picked up the Appalachian Trail yesterday in Harriman and was already looking forward to rejoining civilization in Pawling. He hadn't eaten since the two protein bars he'd wolfed down as the sun was coming up, and he was ready for a real meal. Maybe a cheeseburger or two.

The sound of his footsteps was meditative on the uneven ground, and he looked up at the patches of sky that appeared between the tops of the trees, grateful for the mild warmth of the day. In another month or two, the land out west would be scorched and hardened by the summer sun, rain a precious commodity. He wondered what the weather would be like here.

He'd been working a ranch over in Winnett, birthing cows in the dead of winter, when he'd seen the online job posting for a summer farmhand in Milford, New York. Up to then, he'd never been east of Colorado, but he'd been unaccountably drawn to the summer position at Darrow Farm and, eventually, to the idea of it as an opportunity for a more dramatic change of scenery. After a few emails, one phone conversation in which he'd been surprised to realize Marty Jacobsen was a woman, and a quick check of his references, he'd been hired. He'd started out on foot in March and had never looked back.

He raised his head as the sound of chatter came from up ahead on the trail. A few seconds later, a couple rounded the bend. Bodhi smiled in greeting as they each raised a hand. Their voices quickly faded behind him, and he continued on, shifting his pack and settling it more firmly on his shoulders.

The pack had made countless trips with him across Colorado, Wyoming, and Montana, plus one sweltering summer in Texas, and he'd gotten used to answering the questions prompted by its presence. Old women wanted to know where he was from and truckers asked where he was headed. Kids asked him why he didn't have a car while their parents wondered about his parents. But the one thing everyone wanted to know was if he got lonely. The question had surprised him at first. Being alone wasn't something he feared or even thought about. It was a resting state, as natural as breathing since he'd left home at fourteen without a word to anyone. He'd been careful to stay under the radar right up until his eighteenth birthday last year. If his dad had reported Bodhi missing and he'd been caught, he would have been forced back to the crappy little apartment in Billings. Or worse, into foster care when Child Protective Services realized his dad was a drunk. He was better off on his own, something he'd proven by quickly picking up seasonal labor with the migrants who came north in the summer. He was a good worker, a hard worker, and he soon had a list of farms and ranches that were happy to have him back for the next season.

The winters were the toughest for finding work. Then the farms were all but shut down, jobs hard to come by. Still, he'd always managed to keep a roof over his head, traded for milking cows or feeding cattle, both of which had to be done year round. The barns where he slept offered a kind of continuity; the soft shuffle of animals and the smell of hay and manure were the same everywhere. It was the closest thing he had to home, and he slept deep and sound there whether he was on an apple farm in Wyoming or a cattle ranch in Montana.

He knew what people thought about the fact that he hadn't been to school since he left home. He could see it in their eyes. That he was stupid, a loser. Deep down, he even wondered if they were right. His dad sure had thought so. But the truth was, he never did stop learning, and he had over a dozen library cards from all over the West. The long, cold nights of winter were his favorite. Then he was sometimes the only farmhand on the payroll, and he'd finish chores for the night, sprawl across his bunk, and read until his eyes burned. When the library was too far from the ranches and farms where he was employed, he'd dig around the bunkhouse for whatever he could find, just as likely to come upon a back issue of *Field & Stream* as an old copy of *The Sun Also Rises*. Didn't matter. He read what he could find, and while he knew it didn't make him educated, exactly, he also knew he wasn't dumb.

He'd taken the GED when he was sixteen and changed his name when he turned eighteen. The choice of Bodhi was a little ironic, since he was about as far from enlightened as anyone, but it had a kind of anonymity to it, and he liked the idea of being a faceless wanderer, searching for truth, rather than a former runaway without a single soul to care whether he lived or died. His new last name, Lowell, had been his mother's, and the forgettable nature of it suited his purposes perfectly. He was tall, but not noticeably so, and while his years of ranch work had made him strong, his brown hair and eyes were nothing if not average. It was how he liked it. He was just passing through, had no desire to leave any trace of himself or form any attachments. The truth was, he hadn't had much luck with people. His best interactions with them had come from a distance, and he planned to keep it that way.

Three

The school parking lot was half full by the time Rose pulled her mom's 1968 Chevy into a spot near the front. She was rebraiding her still-damp hair when Will pulled into the spot next to her, his pickup screeching as he turned the wheel.

"Hey, Red," he said, jumping out of the driver's side.

Will was the only one who called her by the nickname. She didn't love it, but she didn't correct him. The farm would have been sunk without him these past few months. He could call her whatever he wanted.

"Hey," she said, wrapping a hair tie around the end of her braid. "Still haven't gotten that belt replaced?"

He shook his head. "Haven't had time."

She raised an eyebrow. "Bet you had time to conquer that new game on Xbox last night."

He swatted at her with the sweatshirt in his hands. "And

time to help you with that bull, too."

The bull was notoriously stubborn about coming in from the north field, and she and Will had spent a half hour on their horses the night before trying to force the animal into its pen.

"Yeah, yeah," Rose said. "You were probably just killing time while your controller charged."

He grinned. "How'd you know?"

She bumped him playfully with her shoulder as they headed across the parking lot. She'd seen him as a gap-toothed kid, an awkward middle schooler, a gangly adolescent. Now he was a man. Okay, maybe not a man, but a guy at least. He didn't miss much, and his blue eyes had only grown clearer and sharper over the years. His blond hair was cut short, and his broad shoulders strained at his T-shirt. She was surprised to realize that he was at least four inches taller than her now.

"That guy Aunt Marty hired is supposed to be here any day. Then I won't need your help as much," she promised.

"I don't mind helping, but I'm glad you'll have someone around to give you a hand when I can't be there."

"Last day of senior year . . ." She heard the note of wistfulness in her voice and wasn't surprised when Will turned to look at her. He knew her better than anyone.

"What?" he asked. "You going to miss the hard-ass chairs? The crappy cafeteria food?"

She laughed. "Hardly. It's just . . . Well, everything's going to change." It wasn't really the truth. Everything had already changed. But high school was one of those places where she could still see her mother, waiting to drive Rose home after school freshman year, walking the halls during Open House, cheering Rose on the one season she'd played volleyball.

"I know what you mean," Will said.

She was grateful he didn't push. And it was more than just her mom. Graduation was Saturday, and then her classmates would be going on to college or trade school, traveling, going to work or into the military. But she would be here in Milford, just like she'd always been, despite the money she'd saved and the shoe box full of travel brochures that she'd been keeping under her bed since she was twelve. She'd go to community college, but it wouldn't really matter. Nothing would change, and she felt the weight of the impending sameness bear down on her like a runaway bull.

It was her own fault. Overwhelmed with her mother's sickness and then her death, Rose hadn't even applied to college. Aunt Marty tried to tell her it wasn't too late, that she could take a gap year, then apply to school next year. But the farm wouldn't run itself, and her dad's grief demanded his full attention. What was she supposed to do? Abandon him? Abandon the farm? She couldn't do either of those things. Besides, it had been so long since she'd been able to think about anything but the farm that she didn't even know who she was without it.

"What does she mean?" The voice came from her left, and Rose turned to see her best friend, Lexie, bouncing next to her, holding her usual Styrofoam coffee cup. Rose had no idea what was in it; could be a nonfat vanilla latte, could be a black iced coffee. Lexie was funny that way. You never knew what she would do or say or wear. "What are we talking about?"

"Graduation," Rose said, looking over her friend's tutu skirt, cowboy boots, and flannel shirt. "And what in god's name are you wearing?"

Lexie gave a toss of her long blond hair. "You know what Grandma Russell says."

Rose groaned at the mention of Lexie's grandmother, whose clichés Lexie pulled out on an almost hourly basis.

"Even marching to the beat of your own drummer isn't an excuse for that getup." Will laughed.

"Just because you two want to look like farmhands all the time doesn't mean the rest of us do," Lexie said.

"You're wearing cowboy boots," Rose pointed out.

"These?" Lexie looked down at the boots. "This is *fashion*. Not function."

"There you go," Rose said, turning to Will. "All we need are tutus and we're good."

Will laughed.

Lexie had moved to Milford three years ago, part of what had seemed like a mass exodus from the city. The town, once strictly rural, had become a mix of old farm families and middle-class commuters looking for the good life. The population had exploded, and the bus routes had gotten longer, the classrooms more crowded as the district tried to figure out how to make it all work.

"Hey, Lexie." It was Travis Shelton, walking backward and grinning at Lexie like they had a secret.

Lexie sighed. "It was just a kiss, Travis." She didn't make any effort to keep her voice down, and a few of the other people heading into the building turned to look at her.

Travis looked hurt. "More than one."

She rolled her eyes and looked away, ignoring him until he faced forward and pushed through the front doors of the school.

"God," she said. "It's like we're engaged or something just because I made out with him at the bonfire."

Will snorted. "You might be getting a little ahead of yourself. He just said 'hey.'"

"Yeah, well, I'd rather shut it down now," she said. "The last thing I need when I go to FIT is a small-town boyfriend holding me back."

Rose laughed, imagining Lexie trying to juggle someone like Travis with her curriculum at the Fashion Institute. "Places to go and people to see, huh?"

"You know it. After this summer, I'm out of here. The city beckons." She looped her arm through Rose's. "And you are coming to visit every weekend. There are tons of hot guys down there."

"I'm not exactly on the market, Lexie."

"That's the perfect time to find someone," Lexie said. "Just . . . you know, get out and let love find you."

Rose raised her eyebrows. "Let love find me? Is that more

of Grandma Russell's advice?"

Lexie sighed. "Okay, so it's a little corny. But it's true."

They headed down the main hall as the first bell rang. "Come on, Red," Will said. "Let's get to calc before Lexie finds a way to pimp you out."

"Sounds good," Rose said. She didn't even have time to condition her hair most days. The last thing she needed was a boyfriend.

Four

Bodhi's first stop was the mini-mart in town. He'd exited the Appalachian Trail near Pawling, stopped for food, and hitched a couple of rides north to Milford. Now he was almost out of water, and he bought five bottles, drinking one and stuffing the rest in his pack before following the cashier's directions to the small library off Main Street. Marty Jacobsen had told him no one would be at the farm until after five during the week. A library was as good a place to kill the time as any.

The library was in an old house off Main Street that had been opened up to accommodate two floors of books. An elderly woman greeted him with a nod, her gaze lingering on his face as he stepped inside. He saw the surprise in her eyes when he headed for the desk.

"Ma'am," he said.

She nodded. "How may I help you?"

He held out his hand. "I'm Bodhi Lowell. I'll be working on the Darrow farm, and I suppose I need to get myself a library card."

She took his hand, her skin cool and papery next to his. "It's nice to meet you, Mr. Lowell! I'm Betsy Rand. I had no idea the Darrows were hiring this season. They usually get by with help from some of the locals. Although . . ." She hesitated before giving him a smile. "Never mind! I can help you with that library card."

She put his information into an old computer and handed him a plastic card. "All of our fiction and nonfiction is on this floor. The children's section is downstairs."

"Thank you." He held up his used copy of *Infinite Jest*. He'd learned not to hold on to things he didn't need. "I don't suppose you have any use for this?"

She leaned over the counter and pointed to a big box in the corner. There was a sign that read DONATIONS on the wall above the box. "We never turn down a book," she said. "Though judging from the overflow here we probably should."

Bodhi dropped his book into the box and browsed the shelves, finally settling on a mystery involving a serial killer. He checked out the book, said goodbye to Betsy Rand, and headed for the Thai restaurant he'd spotted when he'd first made his way into town.

He'd expected a small East Coast town to look different from the western ones where he'd cut his teeth, but other than the lack of mountain peaks in the distance, everything was pretty much the same. There was the Thai place, a couple of gas stations, the mini-mart where he'd bought his water, a pizza joint, a diner, and a strip mall that included a hardware store and a bagel shop. The biggest building in Milford was the Tractor Supply, a giant agricultural warehouse that stood on the outskirts of town. He would need to stop there to get new boots, but that would have to come after food. His stomach was grumbling, and he was already looking forward to the real food he could count on when working a farm.

He took a spot by the window, then ordered a platter of pad thai and one of chicken curry. He ate slowly, enjoying the taste of the food, the feel of the silverware in his hand, the warmth of the restaurant, all hard to come by on the road. When he was done, he strapped on his pack and headed for the Tractor Supply.

Five

Rose cleaned out her locker and waited in the side lot for Lexie, feeling a pang of sadness when she realized it would be the last time she'd drive her friend home after school. Lexie shared a car with her older brother, but he commuted to the local college, and Rose always drove Lexie home when she needed a ride.

She was looking out over the football field when the passenger-side door opened. Lexie climbed up into the truck. "My glutes are going to miss this workout," she said, settling into the bench seat and putting on her seat belt.

"It's not that high," Rose said. "You'll get more exercise walking around the city."

"True."

Rose put the truck in gear and pulled out of the parking lot.

"How's Buttercup doing?" Lexie asked when they were on the main road.

Rose knew Lexie wasn't really asking about Buttercup. It was just a way for her to get around asking the real questions, the hard ones. Questions like "Was your dad up when you left for school this morning? Has he started helping out around the farm yet? Are you okay? Will you ever be okay again?" Rose didn't mind. If the questions were hard for Lexie to ask, they would be a hundred times harder to answer.

"Not good," Rose said. "I haven't weighed her since last week, but she looks too small, and she's still not nursing the way she should."

"Has she gotten better at bottle-feeding?" Lexie asked.

"Not really. I mean, I manage to get a little bit down her before she pushes me away, but it's not enough."

"What about the cage?"

Rose sighed. "I told you; it's not a cage. It's a cattle chute."

Lexie shrugged. "Whatever. Can't you put her in that?"

"I've tried, but she thrashes and stuff. I'm worried she'll hurt herself."

"Well, what else can you do?" She flipped down the visor to reapply her lip gloss.

Rose thought about it. "I can have the vet set up a feeding tube, but I don't want to do it if I don't have to." It was true that her dad was pretty checked out, but if he found out she'd had to call in the vet, there would be talk of selling Buttercup. The farm barely turned a profit thanks to the property taxes on the land. They couldn't afford to keep a high-maintenance animal that might never add to their balance sheet. She didn't like it, but she'd learned to accept it.

Lexie flipped the mirror up and turned to Rose. "But you might have to, right?"

Rose nodded. "Yeah."

"What does Will say?"

"He says to call the vet," Rose admitted.

"And Will knows his stuff?"

"Yeah." Rose pulled into Lexie's driveway and put the truck in park. "But I'm going to try the bottle for a little bit longer. I just have to pick up some more nipples before I head to Marty's."

Lexie held up her hands. "Whoa! Nipples for cows is where I get off." She reached for the door, then turned back, her expression serious. "You are going to visit me in the city, right?"

"Definitely," Rose said.

Lexie looked into Rose's eyes. "Promise?"

"You haven't even left yet. Why are you pushing it?"

"Because if you don't come to the city, I know what will happen to you, and I'll hate it if it does."

Rose smiled. "What are you talking about, Lex? You psychic now?"

"I don't have to be a psychic to know how it'll go," she said.

"I still don't know what you're talking about."

She sighed. "You got a raw deal, Rose. You really did.

Your mom dying . . ." Lexie took a deep breath. "Well, it doesn't get much worse than that. I'm your best friend, and I can't know the half of it."

Rose forced herself to swallow around the tightening in her throat. "What does my mom have to do with anything?"

"It has everything to do with everything," Lexie said. "Before . . . before it happened, you had plans. You were going to college in the city, and you were planning to get into that study-abroad program. You were going to have a life outside of Milford. If you give up on that now . . ."

"What?" Rose said softly. "What happens if I give up on it now?"

"We both know what happens," Lexie said. "You stay here, work on the farm, marry Will—"

"Marry Will?" Rose interrupted. She shook her head. "You're crazy."

"Are you sure about that?" Lexie asked. "Because I don't think I am. I think you'll get stuck. You'll need more help on the farm. He'll step in to help you run the place, and pretty soon, he'll come clean about the fact that he's in love with you. Then what will you do? It's not like there are a lot of guys around here. Not anyone better than Will, at least. He'll just be the obvious choice."

Rose laughed. "Will is not in love with me."

"He is, Rose. He's just biding his time, waiting until it's right. And the thing is, you could do worse. I know that, too."

"So?" Rose asked. "I think you're wrong about Will, but

if I could do worse, what's the problem?"

"The problem is that it wouldn't be what you *want*. It would just be what you accepted. You deserve better than that. And how can you even know what you want when the only exploring you've done is in a twenty-mile radius of home?"

Rose looked down at her hands. "What if I don't want anything else?"

Lexie laughed. "Feed that line to someone who doesn't know better. I've seen your stash of travel brochures. Lie to me if you want. I love you. I can take it." She hesitated, then opened the door. "Just don't lie to yourself." She got out of the car and looked back through the open window. "See you Saturday?"

Rose nodded. "If not before."

She put the truck in gear and backed out of the driveway. Lexie didn't understand. She didn't have a bond to the land, to a family legacy. She didn't have a father who would forget to eat without her. And Will was definitely not in love with Rose. They were friends, good friends. Lexie just didn't get it because she never got to know a guy well enough to become friends. That was fine for her, but it's not how Rose worked. She had only been in one relationship, freshman year. It had lasted two months and involved nothing but hand holding, hugging in the hallways, and exactly two make-out sessions—one at Rhonda Washinski's birthday party and the other behind the bleachers during a football game. Rose hadn't been interested in someone since. She didn't mind.

The farm kept her busy, now more than ever. There would be time later for love.

The problem is that it wouldn't be what you want. It would just be what you accepted.

Lexie's words rang in her ears. She pushed them aside. Staying in Milford was a temporary thing. A way to help out until her dad got back on his feet. She would pick up where she left off when he was better.

She would.

Six

Bodhi was crossing the parking lot when he spotted a small, older woman trying to heave bags of chicken feed into the back of her SUV. She was dragging one of the bags off the flatbed cart and trying to shift it into the trunk when the bag started to slide.

Bodhi jogged the remaining steps between them, reaching for the feed just before it hit the asphalt. "Let me give you a hand with that."

"Oh my goodness! Thank you," the woman said.

They got the bag into the car, and Bodhi set aside his pack so he could load the rest. He considered telling the woman he had it under control, but she had a proud tilt to her chin, her jeans and work boots suggesting someone who liked taking care of things herself. It was something Bodhi understood, and he was careful to let her do a little lifting as they loaded the remaining bags together.

When they were done, the woman closed the trunk. "Damn things have gotten heavier!"

Bodhi nodded. "They seem to, don't they?"

Her laugh was throaty, the laugh of a much younger woman. "Oh, who am I kidding? I'm just getting old." She held out a hand. "Maggie Ryland."

Bodhi shook her hand. Her grip was strong. "Bodhi Lowell."

She eyed his pack. "You passing through?"

"More or less," he said. "I'm working on the Darrow farm for the summer."

A shadow seemed to pass over the woman's eyes. "That poor family. Sweet Rose hasn't been the same since her mother passed. I've brought enough casseroles and pies over there to feed an army, and I suspect she hasn't eaten a single one of them."

Bodhi tried to hide his surprise. He had no idea who Sweet Rose was, although he supposed she could be the niece Marty Jacobsen had mentioned, and Marty hadn't said a word about a death in the family either.

"Oh, you didn't know!" Maggie held a hand to her chest. "Listen to me going on. Been living in this town too long. I've become a blabbermouth like everyone else here. Hardly any point in discretion. Everyone knows everything anyway."

"That's all right," Bodhi said, his mind on the Darrows and their loss. "I'm glad you told me. I'll do what I can to make things easier for them."

Maggie touched his arm. "Of course you will. And look after Rose, if you can. Got her mother's stubborn streak and more on her plate than she can handle. Not a good combination, if you ask me."

Bodhi nodded. "I know what you mean."

"You take care now," Maggie said, heading for the front of the car. "Thanks again for the help."

"My pleasure," Bodhi said. He picked up his pack and watched her pull out of the parking lot. Then he headed for the store.

He'd learned the hard way that it didn't always make sense to haul his work boots around. Usually he knew his employment lineup ahead of time so he could make the judgment call; if he was working within a four-day radius of his current job, he'd spring for a good pair of Red Wings, tie the laces together, and haul them around until the situation demanded he travel light. If he knew he had a long distance to travel to the next job, he'd buy something just sturdy enough to get him through. He'd been through seven pairs of boots in the almost five years he'd been ranching and farming, and he'd gotten good at making the best call for his money. Sometimes he got lucky and found himself in proximity to a farm or consignment store that offered used boots, but more often than not he found himself in a building like the Tractor Supply, browsing the inventory and doing the math. Now he just needed something to get him through the summer. The boots would be too heavy for the kind of walking he'd be doing overseas, and there was no sense spending a lot of money when he'd be leaving them behind.

He spent twenty minutes trying out the different models before he chose a pair of sturdy but reasonably priced Ariats. He paid for the boots, but a look at his watch told him it was only three thirty, so he wandered the store for a bit, stopping to pet a group of rescue kittens housed in a wire cage. He was heading toward the front of the store when he spotted the girl, head bent to a shelf full of calving supplies.

He stopped in his tracks. There was something familiar about the bend of her neck, the long copper braid snaking over one shoulder. He knew this even though he was positive he'd never seen her before. She was biting her lip, reading a box in her hands like it held the key to the universe, and for one crazy minute, he thought she might hold the key to his.

Seven

Rose was glad to be inside Tractor Supply. This was familiar ground. Cattle and chicken feed. Galoshes and all-weather gear. Pitchforks and hay rakes. There were no big questions here, not unless you counted which brand of milk replacer to buy or whether to take advantage of the sale (buy one get one 50 percent off) on calf bottles.

She was reading the box on the nipples they used to bottle-feed, wondering if maybe there was some kind of advice she'd missed that would make it easier to feed Buttercup, when she heard the voice on her right.

"Sometimes they don't like those."

She looked up and was surprised to find a guy around her age standing at her shoulder. His voice had been deep, and she looked past him for a second, half believing someone older had spoken. But it was just him.

"What do you mean?"

He tipped his head at the box in her hands and a lock of dark hair fell over his forehead. "Not sure how much experience you have bottle-feeding calves, but the opening in those is too big for a lot of them that have trouble feeding."

She felt her face flush, though she couldn't be sure if it was because he was sticking his nose in her business or because he was staring at her with eyes the exact color of the soil on the farm, rich and warm in the summer sun. It didn't help that he was tall, taller even than Will, with lean, compact muscle that pulled against the sleeves of his T-shirt even though he was just standing there.

"Well, we've been in the business over a hundred years," she said. "How about you?"

His grin was lazy, and he didn't seem at all put out by the challenge in her voice. "A little less than that."

She nodded and immediately felt foolish. Why did she feel satisfied putting a total stranger in his place?

"I'm just saying," he continued, "a lot of times when the calves have trouble feeding, it's because they don't like the rush of milk. A smaller nipple might be less intimidating, although depending on the animal's age, you might have to undo some of its conditioning. Might not want to feed on anything now."

The guy sounded like he knew what he was talking about, but he wasn't the one who'd brought Buttercup into the world, who'd lost sleep worrying about the calf all these months. Plus, he had a kind of drawl to his voice, not quite southern, but not from around here either. What made him think he knew better than her?

"It'll be fine," she said.

He shrugged. "Just trying to help."

His easy manner got under her skin. Here she was, all flustered and annoyed, and he acted like she'd actually asked for his advice, like he had every right to bust in and force his opinion on her.

"Well, I appreciate it," she said, grabbing three more of the boxes in the same size, "but I think I've got it under control."

"If you say so," he said. She was almost to the register when she heard his voice behind her. "Nice meeting you."

She dumped the boxes on the counter and chatted with Ed, the manager of the store, while he rang her up, forcing herself not to look back and see if the stranger was watching her. She paid with the credit card her dad had given her to buy things for the farm and picked up the paper bag with her purchases.

When she got to the glass doors, she looked at the reflection to see if he was still there. He was gone.

Eight

She was still a little flustered when she got to Aunt Marty's house. The stranger's appearance had set her off-balance, and everything she'd said after that had seemed to come from someone else's mouth. She wasn't used to anyone telling her what to do, and definitely not someone her own age, someone who wasn't even from Milford. Sure, she sometimes asked Will for advice, but the Breiners had been running their dairy farm almost as long as the Darrows had raised cattle. And Will was a friend. He knew Rose, knew the farm and how hard she worked on it.

This guy was like one of those hippie types from the college town across the river. His hair was a little too long for him to be any kind of local, let alone one who knew how to raise cattle. Plus, he'd had a backpack, one of those big ones people carried when they were traveling on foot. He was probably some Kerouac wannabe whose cross-country road trip was funded by his parents. So he was good-looking. So what?

She parked in Aunt Marty's driveway, got a box of strawberries out of the back of the truck, and headed for the house. It was small, more of a cottage, really. Marty had only been living in it since she'd returned from Thailand five years ago, but it was perfect for her. Set outside of town halfway up the mountain to Warrensville, it was situated on two acres that backed up to a wooded preserve. It was quiet, rare even to hear a plane fly overhead. A river ran behind the house, and Rose loved sitting outside with her aunt in one of the big Adirondack chairs, listening to the water rush past as she and Marty talked about everything from school to the farm to books they read. Sometimes they didn't talk at all. Then Rose knew they were both thinking of her mother, remembering all the times they'd spent outside together.

The door was open, the unlatched screen fluttering a little in the afternoon breeze. Rose pulled it open and stepped into the house.

"Hey, it's me!" she called out.

"In the office."

Her aunt's voice carried from the back of the house, and Rose set the strawberries in the kitchen before heading to the tiny room her aunt called an office. She found Marty sitting at the old farm table she used as a writing desk. She was leaning forward, peering at her laptop screen, her long red hair trailing down her back.

"What are you working on?" Rose asked, leaning down to kiss her aunt's cheek.

Marty pulled off her glasses and looked up at Rose with a tired smile. "That article on expats in Chiang Mai. The time difference is killing me."

Rose nodded. Her aunt lived simply on the interest from her savings and the freelance writing work she picked up from various travel magazines.

"It must be nice to talk to old friends, though."

"It is," Marty agreed. "I forget how isolated I am here sometimes."

Rose heard the note of wistfulness in her aunt's voice and felt a moment's panic. Marty didn't like staying in one place too long, and she'd already been back in Milford for five years. How long would it be before she moved on? And what would Rose do if yet another person left her alone?

"It would help if you didn't live out in the boonies," Rose said.

Marty laughed. "Everything here is out in the boonies." She stood up and stretched, and Rose was struck by how young her aunt seemed. She was only two years younger than Rose's mother, but her skin was completely smooth except for a few fine lines around her eyes that made her look like she was always laughing. She had the Jacobsen hair and the Jacobsen freckles, all of which only added to the feeling that she was a kid trapped inside an adult's body. Today, like most days, her slender feet were bare under leggings and one of her patterned tunics. "What did you bring me?"

"Strawberries," Rose said. "There will be blueberries in a few days, and the early tomatoes are almost ready, too."

"Great." Marty slung an arm around Rose's shoulder. "Have time for iced tea?"

"I have to feed the animals," Rose said. "But I can stay for a few minutes."

They talked about graduation as they headed to the kitchen. The ceremony would be outside, weather permitting, and Rose was worried about walking to the stage in heels. How did girls do it without the pointy parts sinking into the grass? She wondered if she could get away with wearing her boots, or even her tennis shoes. She'd have the graduation gown on anyway.

Marty poured them each a glass of iced tea and they sat at the tiny kitchen table. Rose watched as Marty traced a ring around the top of her glass.

"I wish Nana and Pop were still alive," Marty said wistfully. "They'd be so proud of you."

"I wish that, too," Rose said softly.

Both sets of Rose's grandparents had passed when she was young, and she watched sadness shadow Marty's eyes like a swift-moving cloud. She felt suddenly ashamed. Marty had lost every blood relation but her. Rose wasn't the only one hurting.

"How's your dad?" Marty asked, changing the subject.

Rose forced a smile. "He's fine."

Marty tipped her head, like she was disappointed Rose would even try to pull one over on her.

Rose sighed. "I can't even answer the question because I hardly see him. He tries to act like he's been up for hours when I get home from school, but I think he's still sleeping most of the day."

"Is he helping out?"

Rose bit her lip. She didn't want to rat on her dad. Rose's mother had been the love of his life. They'd been high school sweethearts right here in Milford. Their families had been friends, and they'd fallen in love in and around the Darrow farm. Rose didn't blame him for not wanting to see it every day. Rose could hardly stand it herself, and she had seventeen years of memories with her mother instead of the thirty her dad had to live with.

"He does what he can," she answered. "I'm managing the rest with some help from Will."

"Having Bodhi Lowell around this summer will help." Her aunt met her eyes. "But honey, it can't go on like this. You're young, you have your whole life ahead of you. It's not fair for you to give that up."

Rose rubbed at the condensation on her glass. Bodhi Lowell. The intruder. Rose was barely keeping up pretenses with Marty, with herself. How would she do it 24/7 with a total stranger?

"I'm not giving it up," she said. "I'm just putting it on hold."

Marty reached across the table for her hand. "I'm going to tell you something no one else will: a lot of life is about momentum. You let yourself stand still too long, you get stagnant, forget there are other places to see, other ways of thinking and doing things. And the worst part is, you start to lie to yourself. Make excuses why it's just fine to be standing still, telling yourself you didn't want anything different anyway." Marty shrugged. "Maybe it's even true for some people. I don't know. But it's not true for me, and it's not true for you."

Rose only thought about denying it for a second. Marty would just remind her about her collection of travel brochures and the hours Rose had spent asking Marty questions about Thailand and Indonesia and Germany and Czechoslovakia. It was a losing battle. And Marty knew something about the subject; she'd once been married to Larry Fuller. Larry ran the small engine repair shop in town and had been in Milford his whole life. He and Marty hadn't lasted three years. Now he had three kids and was married to a nice woman who ran the PTA. Rose could tell he was happy, and so was Marty.

"The farm isn't your problem. It'll work out somehow," Marty said. "Just promise you'll think about it."

"I will," Rose said. "I promise."

Nine

The truck didn't have air-conditioning, and Rose was hot and exhausted by the time she got home. What she really wanted was a nap, but she had to bring the cows in and get them fed before dinner, so she opted for a quick swim instead. She hurried into the house and changed into her bathing suit, then threw on a pair of worn jean shorts and grabbed a towel on her way out the door.

She crossed the dusty private road that separated the house from the orchard and picked her way across the fallen fruit. The orchard hadn't been a priority for her dad, who preferred working with cattle, and the trees had grown gnarly and wild without regular pruning. There was still enough fruit for Rose to collect for the farmers' market, but the orchard wasn't producing near what it had in its prime. Rose's grandmother had loved it, and in her mind's eye, Rose could still see the ladders tipped against the old trunks, disappearing into the foliage as the farmhands plucked ripe fruit from the branches. Her grandmother would can some of the peaches and use the rest for pie and jam until fall, when it was time to harvest the apples and pears. Then there would be tangy applesauce and warm spice cake, pear tart and fried cinnamon apples, sandwiches with ham and sour apple slices.

She continued through the orchard and over the small knoll at the back of the field. The swimming hole glimmered in the early summer sun, and she ran down the hill shrieking like she had when she was a kid. For a few seconds, she forgot about everything: her mom's death, the farm, her dad. There was just her and the sun and the land she knew like the back of her hand.

Throwing her towel on the ground, she slipped off her shorts and took a running leap from the big rock that was her launching pad, forcing herself not to gasp as the water closed over her head. It was cold, and she was instantly awake. Alive.

She flipped over and floated on her back, her skin turning to gooseflesh as she looked up at the sky and the trees that rimmed the pond, rustling in the breeze like they were telling her a secret. Closing her eyes, she allowed herself to drift, and for once there wasn't a laundry list of things to do running through her head.

She didn't know how long she'd been there when a cloud drifted in front of the sun, dimming the light behind her eyelids. She flipped over and swam to the side of the pond, then dried off and pulled on her shorts.

She wanted to walk back slowly, to enjoy the late afternoon sun and the sound of the crickets, already chirping in the long grass, but the farm chores needed to be done, and she wanted to try one of the new nipples with Buttercup before she dealt with dinner. At least school was officially over, and she'd have a break from homework until she started community college in the fall.

Her hair dripped cool water down her back as she made her way across the orchard. She was getting ready to cross the road when she spotted her dad, sitting on one of the tractors in the big garage out back. Looping the towel around her neck, she headed toward him, already worried about what she would find there.

She had only the smallest of hopes that he was working. Mostly, he went to the garage to think about her mother. At first Rose hadn't understood it. There were lots of places on the farm more steeped in her mom's presence than the garage. But then Rose had passed by a small picture in the den. It had been shoved back into the bookshelf, almost hidden by the row of *Farmers' Almanac*s her dad kept there. Rose had reached for the photograph, pulling it forward, and then she'd understood; it was a picture of her parents, young and smiling, both of them on top of the old tractor that they still used on the farm today. Her dad was sitting in the driver's seat, balancing her mom on his lap. His arms were wrapped around her waist as she held his face between her palms. Somewhere behind her mom's hands, they were kissing.

"Daddy?" she said when she got to the big doors of the garage.

He looked up, his eyes glazed, and for one terrifying minute Rose thought that he didn't recognize her. Then his gaze cleared and he gave her a pained smile. "Hi, honey. How was school?"

"Fine," she said. "What are you doing out here?"

"Oh, you know," he said, climbing off the machine, "just checking out the equipment, making sure everything's running okay."

She blinked as she looked at him, trying to reconcile the man in front of her with the picture she had of her dad in her head. Usually she saw him in the house, after the brightest daylight had faded. Then he looked almost like his old self.

But the sunlight, even softened like it was by the hour, wasn't kind to him, and she noticed that his dark hair had more gray and his face was more deeply etched than it had been before her mom died. His clothes hung on his wiry frame, and his arms, once lean and strong, looked soft and thin.

"Is it?" Rose asked him. "Running okay, I mean?"

"Looks to be." He patted the side of the tractor awkwardly. "Looks to be."

She wondered if he would ask about the animals, about the calves or the heifers, the bull they'd paid too much for last year. He didn't. Just walked over and draped an arm across her shoulders. "Go for a swim?" he asked as they started toward the house.

She nodded.

"How was it?"

"Nice," she said. "I have to bring the animals in from pasture before dinner. Want to help?"

He hesitated, squinting as he looked out across the fields, like they hurt his eyes. "Maybe I will," he said. "I just have some things to take care of in the house first. You get started without me."

She tried not to show her disappointment. It's not that there weren't things to take care of in the house. After six months of neglect, there were things to take care of everywhere. It's just that she knew he was hedging. He wouldn't be back out to help. He'd go inside, maybe grab a beer, lay on the couch or even go back upstairs to the bed he'd shared with Rose's mother. He'd lay there while the sun slanted lower and lower in the sky, the window shades swinging back and forth in the breeze. Rose would eat dinner alone at the kitchen table with her book. Maybe she'd see him before bed. Maybe.

"Okay, Dad," she said. "I'll see you inside."

They parted ways at the back of the house, her dad skirting the garden to the kitchen door while Rose headed for the front of the house and her work boots in the foyer.

She didn't bother changing, just slipped her boots on and headed to the barn in her shorts and bathing suit top. She was almost there when she heard the footsteps behind her.

She turned quickly, thinking it might be Will. But it wasn't. It was the guy from Tractor Supply. The one who'd tried to tell her what to buy for Buttercup.

She shook her head, then crossed her arms over her chest, self-conscious about the bikini top. "What are you doing here?"

He looked down at a piece of paper in his hand, then at the house, before he turned back to her. "Is this the Darrow farm?"

She nodded. "So?" She wondered if it was her imagination that he was fighting a smile.

"So," he said, "I'm Bodhi Lowell, and I'm here to work for the summer."

Ten

At first she'd just been surprised, her face turning one shade paler, the spray of freckles across her nose standing out against her skin. Then she'd buttoned a flannel shirt over her bathing suit top, and told Bodhi to follow her.

Now they were on their way to one of the barns, and it was obvious she was pissed, her pace fast enough to suggest that she wouldn't have been disappointed if she turned around to find him gone. Of course, it wasn't really hard to keep up given that she was a good six inches shorter than him. He just lengthened his stride a little as she forged ahead.

So this was Sweet Rose. He wasn't all that surprised. It was a small world, and he suspected Milford was smaller than most. And what was it Maggie Ryland had said? That Rose Darrow's mother had passed on? He looked at the graceful bend of the girl's neck, slender and fragile atop a spine of steel, and felt a surge of sympathy move through him.

Since she didn't feel like talking, he used the time to get a look at the farm, or what he could see of it at least. The first thing he noticed was the silence. Working farms weren't usually so quiet, what with the roar of machinery and men hollering back and forth across the fields. There was a large pasture across the drive in front of the house and what looked like an orchard across the road, plus a smaller field between the two barns, one of which they were headed for right now. He caught a glimpse of open space at the back of the house and wondered if that was part of the Darrow operation, too. If it was, Marty Jacobsen had been right; they were sorely in need of help.

Rose Darrow walked quickly beside him, her long legs eating up the ground between the house and the barn almost as fast as his. Her braid was wet now and had turned a darker shade of copper, like an old penny.

They came to the bigger of the two barns, and Rose stepped through the open doors and into the shade. Bodhi inhaled, sucking in the familiar scent of hay, the earthy musk of animal fur and sweat.

"Something wrong?" Rose asked. There was a challenge in the question, like she expected an insult.

Bodhi shook his head. "Not a thing. It's like coming home is all."

"What is?"

"All of it," he said. "The barn, the smell."

She seemed to think about that before speaking again. "Come on. I'll show you to the bunk room so you can get settled." She led him past the long, empty galleries on either side of the walkway to a door at the back of the barn. "The animals are still out to pasture. I was getting ready to bring them in when you got here."

"I'll drop my stuff and take care of it."

She stopped at the door and turned to look at him. "There are forty head right now."

"You got a horse I can use?"

"They're in the smaller barn on the other side of the east pasture. Just don't use the black mare in the first stall. She's mine." She bit her lip. "Actually, don't use the palomino either."

He lifted an eyebrow, waiting for an explanation. She didn't give one, and he nodded slowly. "All right."

She opened the door and Bodhi was hit with a blast of cool air. The room was utilitarian, but it was clean and large, and a soft breeze was blowing in from the open window near the bunks.

She looked around. "It's not much, but it stays fairly cool in the summer, and I changed the sheets this morning and left you clean towels."

"It's fine," he said.

She nodded. "The bathroom is to the right, and you can help yourself to the kitchen in the house. The door's never locked."

"Thank you."

An uncomfortable silence descended on the room in the moment before she crossed her arms over her chest.

"Did you know?" There was an accusatory edge to her voice. "Back at the Tractor Supply."

He shook his head. "No, ma'am."

She sighed, obviously exasperated. "Ma'am? What am I? Sixty? You're probably older than me and you're calling me ma'am?"

He tried to suppress the grin that was fighting its way to his lips. "Force of habit with the boss."

"Well, I'm not the boss," she snapped, then seemed to relent. "That would be my aunt Marty."

"Is she around?" he asked. "I should probably introduce myself, let her know I'm here."

"She doesn't live here," Rose said. "I'll let her know you've arrived. I'm sure she'll come by to check on you sometime soon."

"All right."

"Well, I better go. Is there anything else I can get you?"

"I think I'm good."

She nodded. "Cattle are in this barn here. You should find everything where you need it."

"Thank you."

She turned and left without another word, arms still crossed in front of her. Bodhi puzzled over the situation as he watched her go. Marty was the boss. Rose's mother had passed on. But where was Rose's father?

Eleven

She watched from the window of her bedroom as he walked to the little barn. He emerged twenty minutes later riding Mason, her father's chestnut gelding. She felt guilty when she saw the way Mason pranced. It had been too long since he'd been exercised properly.

Bodhi Lowell sat tall and easy in the saddle. She could tell even from the window that he held the reins lightly, that he knew how to ride. So not a hippie Kerouac wannabe after all. A spoiled rancher's son on an introspective road trip funded by Mom and Dad then.

Rose hurried to the window of the guest room as Bodhi disappeared around the house. She was being a brat and she knew it. Forty head was a lot for one person to bring in on his own, especially someone new to the farm. She knew because she'd done it more times than she could count, and she always finished the job exhausted just as the sun was setting. She should have offered to help, should have saddled up Raven and gone along, showing Bodhi parts of the farm as they went. That's what her mother would have told her to do. But his presence rankled for some reason. Maybe it was because of their interaction at Tractor Supply. Or because he seemed completely at ease in what was obviously an awkward situation while she felt strangely mortified. Either way, there was nothing she wanted less than to ride with Bodhi Lowell.

She watched as he herded the animals across the dirt pathway into the barn. It hadn't rained much this spring, and the cows kicked up so much dust as they went that Bodhi was sometimes almost obscured by it. But his face remained impassive, even when he had to holler at the animals to get them to behave.

When the last of the cows disappeared into the barn, Bodhi dismounted and wiped an arm across his forehead to clear the sweat. Rose would have to tell him about the pond, just in case he needed to cool off during the summer. The realization hit her like a sudden, strong wind: This was Bodhi Lowell. And he would be here all summer, walking and riding the farm, working right alongside her, even eating in her kitchen.

She looked at her phone. Seven o'clock. Would Bodhi come into the house for dinner tonight? She hadn't seen a car, and it was too far to walk into town just for a meal. She tried to imagine eating dinner with him, tried to imagine reading her book while he sat across from her doing . . . what? Chewing? Staring at her? Trying to make conversation? She almost shuddered at the thought.

Hurrying from the room, she walked to the half-open door of her parents' room and peered inside. Her dad was lying on the bed, his hands folded over his chest in a posture almost exactly like the one her mother had been in during her wake. Rose had tried not to look, but she'd been expected to be there, to comfort the people who had known and loved her mother, to sit beside her father, very nearly propping him up with her own body when he seemed about to fall over from the weight of his grief.

She swallowed hard against the sudden memory. Her dad was just asleep. She could tell because his chest rose and fell at regular intervals, and his mouth was half open as he breathed. It was one of the few times she was relieved not to count on him for dinner, and she made her way quickly down the stairs, feeling like a thief.

In the kitchen, her gaze landed briefly on her mother's cookbook. She missed her mom's cooking, missed the familiarity of her food, and even more than that, the *feel* of her in the kitchen, a presence Rose could sense as soon as she came inside after doing chores. Her mother's recipes were in the book, some of them going back to Rose's great-grandmother. And while Rose wasn't as competent in the kitchen as her mother, she could follow a recipe. She could open the cookbook right now, make her mother's goulash or chicken marsala, maybe even an icebox cake for dessert.

She left it where it was, opting instead to stand in front of the freezer like she did every other night, choosing from the casserole dishes that had been brought over in the days following her mom's death. There was nothing exotic. Just the frozen meat loaves and tuna casseroles and chicken-and-rice bakes she'd eaten all her life, but somehow they all tasted just a little bit strange. Still, it was easier than facing the cookbook, than trying to conjure her mother's presence out of a bunch of old recipes when Rose knew it wouldn't bring her back. Worse, it would force Rose to face the reality that her mother was gone, and that was something she just didn't need.

The skin on her arms grew cold. How long had she been standing here, staring into the freezer like a zombie? And how much longer before Bodhi came in to make himself food? The thought finally got her moving, and she pulled a half-eaten casserole from the fridge (she had no idea who had made it or what it was, something with noodles) and spooned some onto a plate. She waited impatiently while the microwave heated it up, then took the plate to her room and picked at the food while she tried to do her homework.

Less than half an hour later the front door opened and she heard Bodhi Lowell's hesitant, heavy footsteps in the foyer. She froze, biting her lip as guilt washed through her. She was being ridiculous. She could hear her mother's voice in her head telling her to go downstairs, make Bodhi Lowell feel welcome, show him where everything was in the kitchen. Or better yet, make him something to eat. But she couldn't seem to move. There was all this stuff she was supposed to do. Take care of the farm and the animals, take care of her dad, keep a good face on things for all the people who looked at her with pity and sadness, who wanted to comfort her when she didn't want to be comforted. And now there was this *one more thing*. This playing the nice hostess for Bodhi Lowell. A stranger. A stranger who would, for all intents and purposes, be living with her this summer. And she just couldn't do it. Not now. Not yet.

She just couldn't.

Twelve

There was a partially eaten noodle dish in the fridge and not much else. Milk, some ketchup and mustard, a few oranges already gone soft, some lettuce that had seen better days. He didn't know what to make of it. Farms required a lot of energy to run. A lot of human energy. Most of the places he'd worked had multiple hands on the payroll during the summer. Big dinners and packed refrigerators were part of the bargain. Who was doing the cooking here? And what were they cooking?

It wasn't until he closed the fridge and opened the freezer that he recalled Maggie Ryland's words outside Tractor Supply.

I've brought enough casseroles and pies over there to feed an army, and I suspect she hasn't eaten a single one of them.

The freezer was packed. There were old-fashioned glass

casserole dishes, chipped and well used, and plastic containers with lids. Disposable metal pans topped with foil and labeled with masking tape (Chicken Enchilada Bake—350 degrees for one hour, Beef Stew—pan warm) shared space with obviously repurposed to-go containers. Bodhi was pretty sure they weren't all from Maggie Ryland, which meant the whole town had been keeping Rose Darrow and her father in food. Not that it did much good. From the looks of things, nobody on the Darrow farm was eating much these days.

He tried to imagine what it would feel like, losing a parent you loved. One who loved you. He couldn't. Love was too good and simple a word to describe the way he felt about his father, not to mention the mother he barely remembered. And while he knew there was no guarantee Rose Darrow's relationship with her mother had been a good one, he thought that it probably had been. He could feel it lingering in the air like faded perfume, could see it in the pictures that lined the walls and shelves and in the worn surface of a countertop that had seen plenty of meals and cups of coffee and early-morning conversations.

He closed the freezer and pulled the noodle dish out of the fridge. After a quick search in the cupboards, he found the plates and piled one high with the rest of the casserole. He was getting ready to put it in the microwave when he thought about Rose and her dad. Had they eaten? The house was so quiet. It might as well have been midnight instead of seven thirty. Should he save them some of the casserole? He wasn't sure, didn't know what to do with the strange situation. Then he remembered the overstuffed freezer. He was probably doing them a favor.

While his food was heating up, he poured himself a glass of milk, downed it, and poured another one.

He thought about taking his food back to the bunkhouse, but he didn't want to seem rude if someone came downstairs, so he sat at the wooden table under a window that looked out over an elaborate but slightly overgrown garden. He scanned the plants while he ate, taking in the early tomatoes, many of them still green. Lettuce sprang from the ground in tufts, bordered by leafy herbs and cucumbers, their vines trailing along the ground. He could make out berries on one side of the fence, the red and blue fruit dotting the landscape like forgotten Christmas lights.

He ate quickly and in silence, making a mental note to bring his book in next time he was hungry. When he was finished, he filled the sink with dish soap and warm water and washed his dishes. He dried them with a dish towel that hung on the handle of the stove and put everything but the casserole dish back in the cupboard.

He leaned against the counter, hesitating. It felt weird to just leave, go out to the barn and not say goodnight or thank you or anything else to Rose and her father. Then again, they didn't exactly seem up for conversation. He would talk to Marty, ask her about the routines of the house so he didn't step on any toes.

Pushing off the counter, he made his way back to the

foyer. He closed the front door behind him and stepped out into a warm and slightly humid night. That had surprised him about New York, that it was humid. Not unbearably so, but a lot more humid than out west where everything was either a desert or close enough that it felt like one. He didn't mind the moisture in the air though. It made everything feel a little fresher, a little more alive.

He looked around as he made his way back to the barn. The farm was pretty, a lot greener than he was used to, and the orchard had been a pleasant surprise. He was used to working cattle ranches where cows meant more money than anything else a rancher could raise, and money was king. Most ranchers couldn't see devoting their land to growing apples when cattle would bring a hundred times more money.

The Darrow property was intimate. He was willing to bet the garden had sat outside the kitchen window for decades, and the trees in the orchard had probably been producing fruit for at least as long. He assumed the farm made some kind of money; after all, they'd hired him. But it didn't seem that profit and loss was the number one priority, and that would take some getting used to.

"Everyone settled in for the night?" he asked the cows as he walked past them on the way to the bunk room. They shuffled and chuffed. "Glad to hear it."

He stopped at the doorway of the bunk room and surveyed his quarters. The animals were at the other end of the barn, making the bunk room feel detached from the rest of the farm. It probably hadn't been bad when more than one farmhand was on the payroll, but now the room was heavy with silence, the air cool and still. It felt untouched, entirely devoid of life for a place so teeming with it.

As accustomed as he was to being alone, this was solitude of an altogether different brand.

But he'd become good at making himself at home, and he crossed to the window and opened it wider, letting the summer breeze rush in through the open frame.

Better already.

Motivated by the small change, he emptied his pack before moving on to the bed. He inhaled deeply as he unfurled the sheets. They smelled like lavender and sunshine.

Thirteen

Rose stepped outside the next morning a full hour later than normal. The moon was still visible in the indigo sky, the horizon in the east a haze of pink and orange fire. She felt guilty about sleeping in on Bodhi's first day on the farm, but it was the day before graduation, and finally, she didn't have to worry about getting to school. Still, she hurried to the barn, braiding her hair as she went. The cows would be hungry.

She pulled open the big doors, wondering if Bodhi was awake. It felt weird to step into the barn, like she was walking into his apartment or something. The thought faded from her mind when she saw the empty galleries.

The cows were gone.

"Got them fed and out to pasture," a voice said behind her. "Hope that's okay."

She turned to find Bodhi Lowell leaning against the side of the barn. Gone were the hiking boots, the giant backpack, the cargo shorts. Now he was wearing worn jeans and a white T-shirt that fit him a little too well, his eyes concealed under the shadow of a cowboy hat.

"That's fine," she said. "I'm sorry I wasn't here to help. I'm usually up at four."

"No need for that now," he said. "Not unless we're vaccinating or baling or some such."

She crossed her arms, then uncrossed them, feeling ridiculous. What was wrong with her?

"Any problems?"

"Not a one, though I noticed one of your calves isn't feeding right." He hesitated. "That the one you were buying for yesterday?"

"Yeah."

He nodded, and she braced for more of his advice. He didn't offer any.

"I should probably show you the rest of the farm," she finally said. "Do you still have Mason saddled?"

"Sure do." He said it lazily, like he didn't have a care in the world. How annoying. "Had a feeling I'd be getting the grand tour."

"Good. Let me saddle up and I'll meet you back here in ten minutes."

She hurried outside before she could do something else that would be awkward or stupid. Most likely both.

She headed for the smaller of the two barns, wondering

if it was her imagination that she felt Bodhi's eyes on her back. The big door opened with a creak, and she stepped into the dim interior and leaned her forehead against the battered wood. She was breathing heavily, like she'd been riding hard when all she'd been doing was carrying on a simple conversation with Bodhi Lowell. Is this how it would be all summer? Using every bit of her energy to act normal around Bodhi when something inside her wanted to scream that nothing was normal? That nothing would ever be normal again? She didn't even know what that was anymore.

She let the soft scrabble and snort of the horses, the smell of hay and manure, calm her down, and a couple minutes later she felt more like herself. She was being stupid. *This* was normal. The farm. The animals. The chores. Her dad and Aunt Marty, Will, even crazy Lexie, who might be going to the city but would still be part of Rose's life. It wasn't what it used to be when her mom was alive. But it was her life now. She'd better get used to it.

She moved deeper into the barn, stopping in front of the third stall where her mother's palomino, Coco, stood peering at Rose with sad eyes.

She reached a hand over the wooden gate and stroked Coco's nose. "Hey, pretty girl. How are you?" The horse chuffed a little, lifting her nose in the air. "Yeah, me too," Rose said softly.

She took an apple out of her pocket and held it out to the animal, but Coco just sniffed at it before turning away. Rose sighed, withdrawing her hand and making her way to Raven's stall.

The horse danced a little when she saw Rose, then lowered her sleek, black head to sniff at Rose's middle.

"Hey, beautiful." She held out the apple that Coco had rejected. "I'm guessing you won't turn this down."

The horse took the apple from Rose's hand and was still finishing the piece of fruit when she nudged Rose's stomach a second time.

"Do I look like an apple tree to you?" Rose stroked Raven's sleek nose. "Okay, you're right. I have another one."

She gave the mare the second apple in her pocket, letting her finish it before opening the gate and leading her to the tack room.

A few minutes later she had Raven saddled and ready to ride. She led the horse outside, blinking against the sunlight before hoisting herself into the saddle. She walked the horse over to the cattle barn where Bodhi already sat astride Mason.

"She yours?" Bodhi asked, tipping his head at Raven.

Rose nodded. "Since I was ten."

"She's a beauty," he said.

"Thanks." She nodded toward the drive that ran in front of the house. "Let's start with the property boundaries."

"Lead the way."

She tapped Raven into a trot and heard Mason fall into line behind her.

Fourteen

She started with the big field at the front of the house. They used it to grow the hay and alfalfa that was both feed and an extra source of income. Rose led Bodhi along the perimeter, eyeing the crop with a critical eye. It was a miracle they'd gotten it in at all, and she thought back to the wet, muddy days of April when she had raced the clock—and the weather—with Will and his father. Her dad had made a show of helping from time to time, but his heart hadn't been in it, and his apathy had only depressed and distracted her.

Rose nudged Raven into a gallop as they moved behind the barns to the north pasture. Some of the cows were grazing while others snoozed in the sun. A group of calves frolicked like kids while their mothers looked on with obvious boredom. She pointed things out as they went—the problematic bull (she probably should have told Bodhi about that last night), areas where the fence needed repair, the trees at the forest line that sometimes lost branches during strong summer storms.

The sun was warm on Rose's head, the wind a gentle touch on her shoulders as they crossed the dirt road to the orchard. She slowed down then, giving the horses time to cool off while they picked their way through the trees, trying to keep them from stopping to eat the decomposing fruit that still dotted the ground from last season.

"It's pretty," Bodhi said, his voice finally breaking the silence.

Rose looked over at him. "What is?"

He shrugged. "All of it." He faced forward, seeming to choose his words carefully. "I didn't expect that."

"Thought New York was all graffiti and subways?" she asked him.

He smiled a little. "Something like that."

She led him up the hill that separated the orchard from the pond. When they got to the top, she stopped Raven's progress with a gentle "Whoa, girl."

"This is yours?" Bodhi asked. His eyes were still hidden under the cowboy hat, but she could tell he was checking out the pond.

"Yep. You can use it to cool off whenever. It's about twenty feet deep in the middle, and it feeds into a river that runs behind that stand of trees over there." She pointed to show him in case he wanted to go fishing sometime.

"Water cold?" he asked.

"Cold enough." She could see the interest in his eyes, could tell he wanted to continue down the hill and get a better look. But then they would stop and maybe even dismount. She would have to make polite conversation, something she didn't have to do while they were riding. "Ready to head back?"

His nod was slow. "Sure."

She turned Raven around and let the horse pick her way carefully down the hill, then kept a little space between the two animals, just in case Bodhi got any ideas about making small talk.

They spent the rest of the day in not-very-comfortable silence. Well, she didn't know if he was comfortable, but she definitely wasn't. She was too used to being alone, or with Lexie and Will, who did more than their share of the talking. With Bodhi the conversation was intermittent between long, heavy silences that felt anything but natural, although he seemed perfectly okay with them. She focused on filling Bodhi in on the farm, showing him around the little office next to the bunk room where they kept all their records and did their paperwork, giving him log-in permission for the software they used to track expenses and income, the purchase price and weight of the cattle, and the million other things that had to be recorded to ensure they were profitable.

The sun was sinking in the sky when they finally saddled the horses back up and brought the cows in for the night. She was surprised to find that they herded well together, Bodhi instinctively going right when she went left, both of them moving in a kind of unrehearsed dance that funneled the animals across the road and back into the barn with minimal effort.

Once the cows were settled, they took the horses to the tack room and removed the saddles and blankets, then brushed the animals down before leading them to their individual stalls. Bodhi forked in some fresh hay while Rose checked the water.

When they finally stepped out of the barn, Marty's Prius was parked in the drive. Relief flooded Rose's body. Finally, someone who could take charge, at least for a while. Maybe Marty could make things seem less awkward, bridge the gap that made it impossible for Rose to act like a normal human being with passable social skills around Bodhi Lowell.

"That's my aunt Marty's car," Rose explained as they walked toward the house.

Bodhi tipped his head in understanding, and a moment later Marty stepped out of the front door, the screen banging shut behind her.

"Well, hello there!" She beamed as she came toward them, her long hair pulled back into a ponytail. She shielded her eyes from the sun with one hand. "You must be Bodhi Lowell."

"Yes, ma'am." He wiped his hands on his jeans, then held one out to Marty.

She shook his hand. "Marty Jacobsen. I'm glad you made it."

He laughed low and deep. Rose hadn't heard him laugh

yet, not really, and a matching vibration rumbled through her chest at the sound of it.

"Me too," he said.

"Has Rose been giving you the lay of the land?"

He nodded. "Nice place you have here."

Marty smiled. "It belonged to my sister, Kate, Rose's mother. Now it belongs to Rose and her father."

The mention of her mother made Rose feel like she'd been slapped. She wasn't ready for her mother to be a casual part of the past. She immediately felt ashamed. Marty had been every bit as wrecked as Rose and her dad when her mother died. And wasn't it better to talk about her mother than to pretend like she'd never existed?

"I never had a taste for farming," Marty continued. "Or for staying in one place long enough to grow anything."

"I can understand that." He looked around. Was that longing in his eyes? "Still, must be nice to have a place like this in the family."

"It is," Marty said. "As long as I don't have to do the work."

They both laughed, and Rose shuffled a little, feeling like an intruder.

Marty smiled at her. "Hi, honey. Why don't you and Bodhi clean up while I start dinner?"

Rose tried to hide her surprise. Right. Bodhi would join them for dinner. Tonight and any night it was an actual meal where everyone sat at the table, which granted, wasn't very often these days.

It's not that she didn't want him there. Not really. He was nice enough. But everything still felt raw and exposed, and the thought of letting Bodhi see that—of letting anyone see it—well, it just wasn't something she wanted to do.

"You're making dinner?" Rose asked.

"Don't sound so surprised," Marty said. "I can cook, you know."

Rose nodded. Her aunt Marty was decent in the kitchen, although her food of choice was most often exotic and hard to pronounce. But she didn't come to the house to cook. Or she hadn't since Rose's mother had died, and even before that, she had just sat on the counter drinking wine, laughing while Rose's mother moved around the kitchen making dinner, sometimes from the old cookbook and just as often from memory.

Marty smiled. "Go on then. I'll meet you inside." She turned around and made her way back into the house, leaving Rose standing next to Bodhi, feeling like an idiot at the end of a first date.

"I'm going to put on a clean shirt," Bodhi finally said. "See you inside."

"Yeah, see you," she said. But by the time she got it out he was already on his way to the barn, her words aimed at his retreating back.

Fifteen

Bodhi's mouth watered the whole time Rose and Marty cooked. He offered to help, but Marty wouldn't hear of it.

"You've done your part for the day," she said. "There's lemonade in the fridge. Pour yourself some and take a load off."

The mood had been easy and light, the opposite of the atmosphere between him and Rose while they'd worked. Then Marty pulled a binder from the counter and flipped it open, and Rose suddenly went stiff. She crossed her arms, green eyes flashing.

"You're going to use that?" There was a note of accusation in her voice.

"Yes, I am." The look Marty Jacobsen leveled at her niece made it clear she didn't expect an argument.

Rose pressed her lips into a straight line, like that might

be the only way to keep from giving Marty a mouthful.

"Now help me with this biscuit recipe, will you?" Marty said.

Rose moved woodenly into action and said very little while Marty talked easily, drinking from a glass of red wine while she moved around the kitchen. She grumbled good-naturedly when she made mistakes, which was often enough that Bodhi probably should have been worried about dinner, none of which was coming from the stockpile in the Darrows' freezer. Marty was both out of place and in her element, a tropical flower planted in the desert that does its best to grow anyway.

"I'll go get your dad for dinner," Marty said to Rose when everything was done. "Why don't you and Bodhi put everything on the table?"

"I can get Dad," Rose said.

Marty placed a firm hand on Rose's shoulder. "I've got it," she said softly.

A sigh escaped Rose's lips as she watched her aunt walk from the room. A few seconds later Bodhi heard murmurs coming from upstairs, the soft rise of Marty's voice and an answering rumble from Rose's father. Bodhi glanced around, looking for a way to break the tension.

"Any method to this madness?" he finally asked.

Rose turned her eyes on him. "What?"

He gestured to the food lined up on the counter. "Any specific way you want this on the table? Or should I just have at it?"

Her shoulders sagged a little. "It doesn't matter. Put it anywhere."

They worked together, moving platters of meat loaf, mashed potatoes, corn, green beans, and biscuits to the table. Bodhi could hardly wait to dig in. This was the kind of food he was used to. Stick-to-your-ribs food. The kind of food you looked forward to after a long day wrangling animals and lifting bales of hay. Rose had just set a dish of butter and a jar of honey on the table when Marty returned.

"He's not coming," Rose said flatly.

"Oh no. He's coming," Marty said. There was a thread of steel running through her voice, and Bodhi thought that for all of Marty's lightheartedness, he hoped he never had to tell her no.

They sat down, Rose across from Bodhi, Marty at one end of the table. A few seconds later, an older man with graying hair and a wiry build shuffled into the kitchen.

"Hi, Dad," Rose said.

"Hi, honey." He touched her lightly on the head as he made his way to the chair across from Marty.

Bodhi stood. He could almost see the weight of the world on the man's shoulders.

"John, this is Bodhi Lowell," Marty said. "He's the one I hired to help out for the summer."

Bodhi held out his hand. "Nice to meet you, sir. Beautiful place you've got here."

John Darrow took his hand, gave it a half-hearted squeeze. "Thank you."

Marty smiled. "Why don't you sit down, John?" she suggested.

John sat, his eyes moving listlessly over the food spread out on the table. "Looks good," he said.

"I have to say I agree with you, sir," Bodhi said, trying to make conversation. He waited to see if they would say grace. Instead, Marty raised her glass in a toast.

"To new friends."

"New friends." It was a funny kind of chorus. Bodhi enthusiastic, John barely audible, Rose a little annoyed. Or was that his imagination?

Marty talked about her travels while they ate, sharing stories from Thailand and Indonesia, Germany and Holland. It was the best conversation he'd had in a while, and he took full advantage of the opportunity to ask her questions about all of her experiences.

"Have you ever been overseas?" Marty asked as she was clearing the table.

Bodhi shook his head. Should he tell them he was planning a trip at the end of the summer? He wasn't sure. It felt too personal. In fact, he realized he hadn't yet told a soul about his plans. He had guarded it like a secret, like deep down he was afraid someone might try to stop him from starting over. He was still puzzling over this when Marty spoke again.

"Well, you should definitely go," Marty said, running water over the plates and setting them in the sink. "It's life altering. Rose has always wanted to travel, you know."

He looked at Rose, sitting next to him with a faraway look in her eyes. "Where do you want to go?"

She shot a glare at her aunt's back. "I don't know. It's just something I've thought about. You know, a someday kind of thing."

He nodded slowly, wondering why it felt like she was lying and why she would bother about something so minor.

"I think I'm going to read for a bit," John Darrow said, rising from his chair.

Marty turned around. "But I have cherry pie! I bought it from Marie, but still . . ."

"Save me a piece," John said. "I'm doing some research on the weather this season."

"Okay, then . . . ," Marty said.

"It was nice to meet you, Bodhi. Please make yourself at home, and let us know if there's anything you need."

Bodhi stood. "Thank you, sir."

John stopped to kiss the top of Rose's head on his way to the stairs.

"Night, honey."

"Night, Dad."

A leaden silence fell over the room in the moment before Marty clapped her hands.

"Pie! It's time for pie." Her voice was unnaturally bright as she opened the bakery box on the counter. She had just set it on the table when the front door opened and a voice called through the house.

"Does my nose deceive me or has someone been cooking?" It was a boy's voice, followed by the sound of footsteps on the wood floors.

"In here!" Rose called.

A tall blond guy appeared in the doorway holding two gallons of milk, one in either hand. He was thin, but his arms had the muscle of someone who wasn't a stranger to a hard day's work. His eyes went straight to Rose, and Bodhi knew he wasn't imagining the light in the guy's eyes when he looked at her.

He grinned. "Thought I was in the wrong house for a minute."

Rose laughed. "Very funny. You can drop the milk and leave if you're just going to insult me."

The guy laughed, but his smile faltered when his gaze came to rest on Bodhi.

Bodhi stood, and Rose followed suit, looking flustered, like she was surprised he was still there.

"Will, this is Bodhi Lowell, the hand Marty hired for the summer." She turned to Bodhi. "This is Will Breiner. His family runs the dairy farm on the other side of the pond. He's helped out a lot since . . . over the past few months."

Bodhi held out his hand. Will looked at it like it might be some kind of trick, then took it and gave it a quick, hard shake.

"Glad to meet you," Bodhi said.

Will gave a clipped nod. "You, too."

"Nice of you to help the Darrows out."

"It was no trouble at all," Will said. "Rose and her family are my family."

Marty brought the pie to the table. "Will's just being nice.

I'm sure he'll be happy to know he is officially relieved of duty."

Will shifted on his feet before finally taking the milk to the fridge. "Always here to help, Marty. You know that."

"Yes, I do," Marty said, turning her smile on him. "And I appreciate it."

"Stay for pie." Rose spoke suddenly, like she'd been fishing for just the right thing to say and finally landed on the perfect sequence of words.

"Yes, stay," Marty said. "We can't eat it all by ourselves." She seemed to think about that. "Well, we *could*, but it wouldn't be a good idea."

"That's okay," Will said. "I should go. Graduation tomorrow and everything . . ."

Marty's face lit up. "That's right!" She turned to Bodhi. "You should come! We're going out to lunch afterward, and the weather's supposed to be really beautiful."

Rose looked horrified. "Aunt Marty, I'm pretty sure Bodhi doesn't want to spend his Saturday at the high school graduation of someone he doesn't even know."

"I wouldn't want to intrude," Bodhi said.

"You wouldn't be intruding," Marty said. "You're welcome to join us. It's outside on the football field. No tickets required."

"I'll stay and look after things here. You enjoy the day." He could almost feel the relief wafting off Will's body.

Marty was dishing the pie, setting generous slices of golden pastry oozing dark red cherries onto dessert plates with little flowers around the border. She looked up. "Will?"

He shook his head. "I really do have to go. But thanks."

Marty grinned. "More for us."

Will turned his gaze on Rose. "Text me later?"

Rose nodded, and for a split second Will met Bodhi's eyes, like he wanted to make sure the message had been delivered.

See how close Rose and I are? We even text each other at night. We're family.

Bodhi got it loud and clear. He just didn't know why the message stuck in his throat as Will retreated toward the front door.

Sixteen

Bodhi lay in the dark for a long time after he returned to the bunkhouse. He'd said his good nights, taken a shower, and climbed into bed with his book, expecting to be asleep in minutes. Instead he thought about the Darrows. About Rose's dead mother, her missing-in-a-different-way father, Marty with her easy laugh. And Rose. He didn't want to admit to thinking about Rose. There was no reason at all why she should interest him.

First of all, she was the boss's daughter. Or niece. Actually, she was kind of like the boss herself, if you wanted to get right down to it. But also, she wasn't exactly friendly. It was true that he felt a weird kind of familiarity with her, a kind of comfort, but it definitely wasn't mutual. Probably because she looked at him and saw a loser. A guy about her own age who hadn't even officially graduated from high school, who was basically a drifter with no plans for the future, nothing to offer. And why should he feel a connection with her anyway? Because they'd both lost their mothers, albeit in very different ways? Because, like him, it seemed Rose was struggling to make the most of what she had, when deep down she wanted so much more?

He flipped his pillow over and repositioned his head on the cool pillowcase. He was being dumb. He couldn't know that about her. This was her family's farm. For all he knew, she loved it and never wanted to leave. He didn't know her at all. She didn't know him, either, and if she did, she wouldn't like what she found out.

Will Breiner had stuff to offer. He had a neighboring farm and history with Rose's family and friendship with Rose herself. He'd presumably been around when Rose's mother had died, had helped her through it.

Why was he thinking about Will? What did he have to do with anything? It's not like Bodhi actually believed he had a shot with Rose Darrow. Or like he even wanted one. This was a summer job. The last punch on his ticket to a new life. He didn't want to form attachments. He was just in a weird mood. In that place where his body was fatigued but his mind was racing. He'd settle in here, and then it would be like any other job.

The moon was blue-white, shining in through the lone window, leaving a pillar of light on the floor of the bunk room. He thought about the Darrow house, how intimate it had been having dinner with just Rose and her family.

Usually dinner on a farm was a crowded affair. Bodhi might be one of five or ten hands, all gathered around a table in the bunkhouse. Even when dinner was shared with the owners of the farm, the table was crowded, with stories ranging from drunken brawls to girlfriends back home to other jobs.

But tonight had been different . . . special, in a way. He'd been given a glimpse at life inside the family. Not the facade put on for neighbors and friends, but the real deal. He'd seen the tension between Rose and Marty over the cookbook Marty had used to make dinner. Had watched as John Darrow tried to put a good face on what was obviously serious depression. He'd seen Rose's face fall when her dad passed on dessert, had been party to Marty's carefree laughter. And under it all he'd felt their bond, the deep current of family and history that bound them together. It was a little disconcerting to be a bystander to so much honesty, to something so foreign and out of reach.

He thought about Rose, settling into bed in the house, the gentle ticking of the big grandfather clock like a lullaby, probably a small light left on in the kitchen in case anyone got up for water.

What was wrong with him?

He sat up in bed. The bunk room suddenly seemed lonely and barren, and he got out of bed and walked out into the barn, peering up into the rafters. When he found what he was looking for, he made his way to the ladder and climbed, stopping at the second-to-last rung.

The hayloft was fairly big, dusty but otherwise clean.

There were a few bales against the far wall, and some of the dried grass had made its way onto the floor. It only took him a few seconds to make up his mind.

He hurried back down the ladder and headed for the bunk room. He stripped the mattress and pulled it off the frame of the bunk, then dragged it out into the barn. Getting it up the ladder wasn't easy, but if there was one upside to a twin-size mattress it was that he could just manage to shove it up ahead of him, balancing it on his head or shoulder when it threatened to fall to the floor below. He was sweating by the time he finally tipped it into the loft, but he knew immediately it had been the right thing to do.

He spent the next hour remaking the bed and bringing up the rest of his stuff. There wasn't an electrical outlet, but there was one not too far below in the vaccination room. He would go into town tomorrow and buy an extension cord and some kind of lamp.

It was after midnight when he finally settled back into bed, his nose filled with the smell of the barn, so different from the cold concrete and drywall of the bunk room. Here he could smell the heat that had been trapped in the old barn beams during the day, like a fire that had long since been put out, and the musky scent of the animals below. Their occasional shuffle and snort was a comfort, and he put his arms behind his head and sighed. He looked up into the rafters, determined to think of something besides Rose Darrow while he fell asleep.

For a while it worked. He turned over the things he'd

tackle on the farm while the Darrows were at Rose's graduation, the ways he could help lighten her load around the farm, tactics he could try with the little calf, Buttercup, that Rose was so worried about.

He was drifting off to sleep when he realized that every single one of those things came back to her. Rose. Her face was the last thing he saw before he fell into darkness.

Seventeen

"Are you serious right now?" Lexie asked, hands on her hips.

Rose let the graduation gown drop to the ground, already sorry she'd tried to adjust her dress in front of Lexie. "What?"

"You're wearing your *boots* to graduation?"

"They're comfortable!" Rose laughed. "Besides, I'm not sure you're allowed to comment."

Confusion shaded Lexie's eyes. "Why not?"

"Did you look in the mirror before you left the house?"

Lexie looked down at her outfit, partially hidden under her unzipped gown. "Florals and stripes are in this year."

"Together?" Rose asked.

"Yes, together!" Lexie said. "Geez! Pick up a *Teen Vogue* sometime, why don't you?"

"I'll pass," Rose said with a smile. "I like my boots. And I like your stripes and florals, too. I wouldn't want you any other way."

"Aw, Rose!" Lexie's face broke into a smile, and she leaned in for a hug. "I feel the same! Even with those stupid, dirty boots!"

Rose laughed. "Thanks. I think."

They were standing in the gym, waiting for the signal to line up for the walk outside. Rose's dad and Aunt Marty were already out there, probably baking in the early morning heat and shifting on the crappy metal chairs put out for the audience.

The room was buzzing with excited conversation, squeals, and laughter. Friends leaned together to take selfies or lined up in front of the bleachers to get group shots. It was all a little surreal, and Rose wished the day was already over, that she was back home helping Bodhi mend the fence in the north pasture.

Not that she wanted to hang out with Bodhi. More that she just wanted to be home where she wasn't expected to smile and be excited, where she didn't have to see all the other moms sitting in the audience, smiling and crying.

"This is it!" Lexie said, breaking into Rose's thoughts. "By lunchtime, we'll be high school graduates, real adults."

"Yeah . . ." Rose tried to smile.

"Yeah? That's all you have to say?" Lexie asked, her voice soft. "Can't you feel it, Rose?"

Rose shrugged. The tag on her gown was scratching the back of her neck, and the lipstick she'd worn in deference to the occasion made her lips feel simultaneously goopy and chapped. She pressed them together, trying to get rid of the sensation. "Feel what?"

Lexie sighed, then seemed to fish for words before she spoke. "It's like . . . expectation, I guess. Like when we were standing on the edge of that cliff at Minnewaska."

Rose could picture it. They'd gone hiking at the nature preserve with Will last summer, had stood on the precipice of a rocky cliff that descended to the glacial lake below. It had been scary and exhilarating, the long drop, all that space in front of them.

"Only this time we can jump, and we won't fall," Lexie continued. "We'll fly."

Would they, Rose wondered? Would they fly? There had been a time when she had felt the invisible safety net of the whole world beneath her. When it had seemed impossible that anything truly horrible could happen. You were young, you had your family and friends, everything always worked out in the end.

But then her mom had died, and if that didn't prove that everything didn't always work out in the end, what did?

"I guess," Rose said.

Lexie opened her mouth to say something, then seemed to change her mind. A few seconds later, she smiled conspiratorially. "Let's talk about something else. Like that guy you're shacking up with."

Rose sighed. She'd texted Lexie the night Bodhi arrived and had been giving her updates ever since, but that didn't mean she wanted to talk about him here, in front of the entire senior class.

"I am not 'shacking up' with a guy," Rose said. "He's working on the farm, and that means he has to live there.

But I told you: I think he's older than us, and his room is in the barn."

"Yeah, for now." Lexie's smile was full of meaning that Rose didn't want to decipher.

"You're being ridiculous."

"Just tell me if he's hot," she said. "You said he was young!"

"That doesn't mean he's hot." Rose laughed.

"Yeah, but he is, right?"

Rose was trying to find the words to describe Bodhi in a way that would satisfy Lexie without making it seem like she'd spent too much time looking at him when someone spoke behind her.

"Who is what?"

Rose turned. It was Will. She opened her mouth to answer, remembering the weird look on Will's face when he'd seen Bodhi in her kitchen. Lexie's words floated through her mind.

He'll step in to help you run the place, and pretty soon, he'll come clean about the fact that he's in love with you.

But it wasn't true. She knew it wasn't. Will was just protective, that's all. Like a brother. Still, she didn't want to talk about how hot Bodhi was around Will, and she could only hope Lexie felt the same way.

"I was just asking Rose if the new farmhand was helping out," Lexie said.

Whew.

"Is he?" Will asked, looking into Rose's eyes.

"Is he what?"

Will raised his eyebrows. "Helpful?"

"Right," Rose said. "Yeah. I mean, he only got here a couple of days ago, but he seems to know his way around a farm."

"That's good," Will said. "I was surprised he's so young. What is he? Around our age?"

"Maybe a little older," Rose said. "We haven't talked much."

"You sure he has the experience you need on the farm?" Will asked.

Rose shrugged. "Marty hired him. I'm sure she checked him out."

Will nodded. "Well, I'm right across the field if you need anything."

"Thanks," Rose said, smiling.

"Let's take a picture!" Lexie suggested. "This is the last hour we'll all be in high school together."

Rose stood between Lexie and Will, and Lexie took the picture with her phone. A couple of seconds later their principal, Mr. Finnemore, shouted for them to line up. After that, there was the long procession out to the football field, the sun hot and bright after the fluorescent lighting in the gym. She spotted her dad and Aunt Marty in the audience as she made her way to her seat. Marty waved, and Rose thought she saw the glimmer of tears in her dad's eyes. It made her own eyes water. Was he missing her mom, too? Wondering what she would be wearing and saying, how proud she'd be on this day, the end of a journey they'd started together?

Rose had to swallow the lump in her throat as she continued to her seat. Then it was a series of speeches and announcements and awards. It only started sinking in when Mr. Finnemore started to call their names. Lexie was right. This was the end of something, and the beginning of something, too. Rose just wished she knew what it was, that she could fast-forward to a time in her life when she knew how it all turned out.

They called her name, and she walked to the podium to get her diploma. She passed Marty, crouched up by the makeshift stage so she could get better pictures, then froze when Mr. Finnemore handed her the diploma so Marty could get the shot. She returned to her seat, where she waited out the rest of the ceremony.

Finally, it was over. Will was out of sight, but Lexie flashed her a smile from across the lawn and they both threw their caps into the air on cue. Then everyone was hugging and laughing and trying to find their parents. Rose stood in the press of bodies, the diploma heavier than it should have been in her hand, a reminder that she was supposed to know what to do next, that she was supposed to have a plan. She thought of the farm. The quiet of it, the solitude. And suddenly all she wanted was to be riding Raven across the north pasture, Bodhi Lowell a strong and silent presence beside her. Which didn't make sense at all.

Eighteen

She changed into shorts right when she got home, happy to be out of her sundress, even though it was a lightweight floral that was pretty comfortable once she'd ditched the cap and gown.

They'd gone to lunch after the ceremony, ending up at Sweet Clementine's like everybody else in town. Clementine's was a little café owned by Marie LeMarche, a pretty, dark-haired woman whose family had helped found Milford in the 1700s, and named after Marie's five-year-old daughter. If you wanted something nice, Clementine's was the only game in town, and the place had been brimming with a post-graduation crowd in high spirits. Rose's family had ended up pushing tables together with the Breiners, and a couple of times she'd looked up to find Will staring at her. She had the sense of a subtle shift in the terms of their friendship, although she had no idea what it meant.

It was a relief to be back on the farm, and she walked out to the barn, expecting to find Bodhi working on last month's balance sheet, getting familiar with their software. He wasn't in the office, though, and the balance sheet was open on the computer, the columns filled in and complete. She walked between the empty galleries—the cows would be out to pasture now—wondering if Bodhi was taking a nap. She wouldn't blame him. Farm hours sucked most of the time.

But when she opened the door to the bunk room, he wasn't there. Even more surprising, the mattress on his bed was gone. She looked around the room. His stuff was gone, too. Had he left? Decided the Darrows were too crazy or depressed for him? She knew instinctively that wasn't right either. She didn't know much about Bodhi Lowell, but she suspected he wasn't the type to disappear without explanation. Besides, you didn't usually take your mattress when you were trying to make a clean getaway, did you?

She made another pass through the barn, then went outside and scanned the fields. No sign of him. There was only one other possibility, and she headed for the horse barn, not at all surprised to find that she'd been right; Mason was gone.

She gave Coco a quick nose rub, feeling bad that she didn't have an apple in her pocket even though the horse probably wouldn't have taken it, then saddled up Raven and headed for the orchard. She felt like she could breathe for the first time all day. The air was soft and warm, the farm alive with birds and the soft call of the cows in the back field.

She navigated Raven through the trees and ascended the hill leading to the pond. At the top, she pulled the horse to a stop. Mason was tied to a tree while Bodhi lay on the grass next to the water. Her breath caught a little at the sight of him, bare chested, his arms behind his head. She couldn't see his face, but she knew from his look of contentment that he had his eyes closed.

"You going to come down?" he called without moving a muscle.

She looked around, thinking he was talking to someone else. But no, it was just her. How had he known she was there?

"Um . . . yeah. I thought maybe you were sleeping." She gave Raven a nudge and they started down the hill.

"You in the habit of watching people sleep?" he asked, his eyes still closed. The heat that rose to her cheeks had nothing to do with the sun. He must have read something into her lack of response, because he sat up then, looking at her with a grin. "I'm just giving you a hard time."

She stifled a sigh of relief. He was letting her off the hook. "We just got back."

He peered up at her, shielding his eyes from the sun. "So it's official then? You're a high school graduate?"

She nodded solemnly. "I'm afraid so."

He laughed a little. "Have a seat. Or better yet, take a dip. Can't think of a better way to celebrate."

She hesitated. She didn't have her suit, but she might as well sit. This was what she'd wanted, wasn't it? A quiet moment on the farm?

And time with Bodhi Lowell, a voice whispered in the back of her head.

She pushed it aside and dismounted, then tied Raven to a tree next to Mason.

She walked over to Bodhi and sat next to him, careful not to sit too close.

"How was it?" he asked.

She looked at him. "The truth?"

"Always."

"Long. Boring."

He nodded. "I've never been one for ceremony myself." He looked out over the pond. "This is more my speed."

"Me too," she said.

"Then again," he started, "sometimes I think we should celebrate every chance we get. You know?"

The rest of his words were unspoken, but she could feel them hanging in the air. *Because life is hard and tragic. Because anything can happen, and you know that better than anyone.*

Adrenaline coursed through her body on the heels of something she couldn't quite define. Anger? Annoyance that he thought he knew her? That he thought he was allowed to reference her mother's death, even subtly? She didn't know.

She stood. "I have to go."

He stood up too fast, almost knocking her over with his proximity.

"Rose, wait." They were only inches apart now. She could see a few drops of water still beading on his chest, could see the rise and fall of it, like he was breathing hard and fast. "I didn't mean . . . I wasn't trying to say . . ."

For a minute she was locked in the warmth of his eyes, afraid to move in case she accidentally brushed against him, in case they ended up even closer and she decided she didn't want to leave at all.

"It's fine." She finally choked out the words. "I just have to go." She headed for Raven, stepping into the saddle and swinging her leg over the horse. "Want me to help bring the cows in?" she asked once she was a safe distance away.

He shook his head. There was something sad in the set of his shoulders. "I got it. Enjoy the rest of your day."

She turned away, kicking Raven into a trot. She didn't breathe easy until she was almost back to the barn, Bodhi Lowell well behind her.

Nineteen

Bodhi was unaccountably nervous as he changed to go into town. It had been two days since his conversation with Rose at the pond, and he was still kicking himself. She seemed to have forgotten about it, but he couldn't believe he'd been so stupid. She was skittish, afraid to let anyone get close, like one of the wild horses he'd seen in Nevada that ran if you came within twenty feet of them.

He should have kept it light, not tried to be all philosophical. And the funny thing was, he hadn't even been talking about Rose and her mom's death. Not really. He'd been talking about himself. About how few occasions there had been to really celebrate in his life. Not that he felt sorry for himself. You played the cards you were dealt, plain and simple, and you played them the best you could. He'd done that. Was doing it. But it seemed to him that if you had cause to dress nice, to smile and be happy, to take just a minute and say to yourself, *Right now everything is good*, well, that might be the thing to do.

Then again, what did he know?

Besides, it was for the best. At the end of the summer, he'd be on a plane to Europe and Rose would be here, probably looking for another person just like him to help out for the fall. And it's not like he wanted something permanent anyway. He'd had some experience with girls. He hadn't exactly been sheltered. But his relationships—if that's what you wanted to call them—had been simple and brief, lasting only as long as whatever job he was working. His nomadic lifestyle didn't lend itself to long-term commitment, and that had always been just fine with him.

Rose deserved better. Someone who would stay and help with the farm. Who had something to offer. Like Will Breiner.

He buttoned his jeans and walked to his duffel to look for a clean shirt.

"Bodhi?"

The voice came from beneath him in the barn. He froze, wondering if Rose would mind that he'd moved into the hayloft.

"Up here," he called out. "One sec."

He had just pulled a shirt from his bag when Rose spoke behind him. "What the . . ."

He turned, still holding the shirt. "Hey, sorry. I didn't know you were coming up." Her eyes were locked on his bare chest, and he hurried to put his shirt on.

She finally looked away, scanning the rest of the room. "Did you move up here?"

"Yeah. I hope you don't mind."

"Why would I mind?"

He shrugged.

"I just . . . are you sure? There's no furniture, no outlets . . ."

"That's why I asked for a ride into town," he explained. "Thought I'd pick up a few things."

They'd been running through the list of upcoming vaccinations when Rose had mentioned that she was going to town. She hadn't seemed to mind when he asked for a lift.

"You didn't like the bunk room?" she asked.

"It was fine," he said. "I just . . . I don't know how to explain it."

Her expression seemed to soften a little. "Try," she said quietly.

He was surprised. That she was talking to him like this, that she wanted to know at all. "That night at dinner, with Marty and your dad and . . . you?"

She nodded.

"It was nice. Warm. Homey." He shrugged. "The barn is home to me."

"This barn?"

"Any barn."

She studied him for a minute and he felt suddenly self-conscious. He sat on the bed, avoiding her eyes as he put on his boots.

"You should have asked for help with the mattress." She surprised him again by laughing a little. "Must have been hard to do it yourself."

He stood, a smile rising to his lips. "It wasn't easy."

She bit her lip, like she was trying not to laugh again.

"Something funny?" he asked.

She giggled. "It's just funny to imagine, that's all."

"I'm glad I can entertain you." And the funny thing is, he meant it. It was the first time he'd really heard her laugh. It was subdued, careful, but it was there.

"Well, I guess I see why you need to go to town," she said.

"Yeah, this place needs a little something."

She headed for the ladder. "I'll say."

He followed her down and they made their way to the old Chevy parked in the driveway.

"Nice truck," he said, getting in.

She fired up the engine and paused, her hands on the wheel. "It was my mother's."

He hesitated. "It suits you."

She looked over at him. "You think so?"

He nodded.

She smiled a little and put the truck into gear.

The farm was about five miles outside of town. They passed rolling fields set against a ridge of mountains in the distance. He focused on the scenery to avoid looking at her, afraid if he did he wouldn't want to stop.

They pulled into a spot in front of the grocery store. Rose turned to him. "I have to get some things for the house.

There's a consignment store on Main Street that usually has lamps and stuff, and the hardware store should have an extension cord. Do you want to take the truck and meet me back here when you're done?"

"I'll walk," he said. "It's nice out. Just head over when you're done here."

"Sounds good." She hesitated. "Any special requests from the store?"

Did this mean she would be cooking? They were still fending for themselves, living off the stockpile of food in the Darrows' freezer. She was never in the kitchen when he went in for a meal, and he'd spent every night since the dinner with Marty reading alone at the table while he ate.

"I'm not picky," he said.

She nodded and got out of the car. He watched her pull a list from her bag and disappear inside the store. Then he turned and headed for Main Street.

Twenty

He stopped at the hardware store and picked up an extension cord, a broom, a couple of hooks for his clothes, and a plastic bin to keep everything else organized. He'd just leave it all behind at the end of the summer.

He carried his purchases to the consignment store and propped them next to the door of the shop. Milford didn't strike him as a place you couldn't leave something for fifteen minutes for fear it would be stolen.

A bell rang over the door when he entered, and he scanned the shadowy interior, his gaze resting on what looked like a dresser in the back of the store. He was heading that way when a familiar voice stopped him in his tracks.

"Well, hello again!"

He turned toward the counter to find the older woman he'd met at Tractor Supply when he'd first gotten into town.

"Hello." He crossed over to the counter.

She smiled. "Maggie Ryland. Remember? We met the other day."

He nodded. "Yes, ma'am."

"How are you?" She seemed genuinely happy to see him, the wrinkles around her blue eyes etching deeper as she smiled.

"I'm just fine, thank you."

"And how are you finding the Darrow farm?"

"It's . . . nice."

One eyebrow shot up. "A little rough over there still?"

"A little," he admitted, not wanting to say too much.

Maggie nodded sadly. "I'm sure it's a help to Rose to have you there."

"I hope so," he said.

"She's a lovely girl, our Rose," Maggie went on.

He shifted a little on his feet, not sure how to answer. "Yes, ma'am."

"I'm sure she's happy to have some company."

"I'm happy to help," Bodhi said carefully.

Maggie gave him a knowing smile. "I'm sure." She gave the counter a light slap. "Now, what can I do for you? This place is quiet as a tomb most days. You have no idea how happy I am to see you!"

Bodhi laughed. "I'm looking for a few things for my room at the farm."

"I'm sure I can help with that," she said, coming around the counter. "And you'll be helping me get rid of some of this junk!"

Bodhi followed her to the back, and by the time Rose came through the door forty minutes later, he'd acquired a lamp, a small side table, an old rug, and some books for less than twenty dollars.

"Wow . . . you set him up, Maggie," Rose said, eyeing the purchases on the counter.

Maggie grinned. "Can't have such a nice boy going without, now can we?"

There was a twinkle in her eye that made Bodhi nervous, like she was a favorite aunt trying to set him up on a blind date. Not that he had any favorite aunts.

"I guess not," Rose said.

"Are you sure I can't give you more for all this?" Bodhi asked.

"I should be paying you," Maggie laughed. "Honestly, this place is just a hobby. I don't like to be idle, you know."

Bodhi grinned. "I got that impression."

"I'll start loading this stuff into the truck," Rose said. She picked up the lamp and an armful of books and headed outside. The bell on the door jingled as she left.

"Tell me," Maggie said softly, "is she okay?"

Bodhi didn't like gossip. He'd been in enough small towns to know that it was insidious, and even seemingly harmless bits of information could be hurtful if divulged to the wrong person. But he heard the kindness in Maggie's voice, knew instinctively her question was based on concern, not idle curiosity.

"Hard to say," Bodhi said. "She doesn't talk much."

Maggie's nod was slow. "Wasn't always that way. Used

to see her around town with her mother—spitting image, by the way—smiling and gabbing like best friends."

Bodhi's eyes drifted to the glass door. He could see Rose arranging the lamp and books in the cab of the truck.

"Looks too thin, too," Maggie continued.

Rose came through the door a second later and folded her arms. "So I'm driving and hauling?"

Bodhi sprang into action, picking up the side table and the rug. "Sorry." He turned to Maggie. "Thank you, Ms. Ryland."

She clutched at her throat. "You'll have to call me Maggie if you don't want me to feel a million years old."

Bodhi laughed. "You got it. Thank you, Maggie."

"You're welcome." She turned her gaze on Rose. "I have some fresh chickens in the fridge, and I know how much a boy this age can eat. I'll have to have you both over for dinner, and your father, too, of course."

Rose smiled. "That would be nice."

"I'm going to remember you said that," Maggie said.

Bodhi hoped Rose intended to accept her future dinner invitation, because he had a feeling Maggie would be calling to extend it sooner than Rose expected.

"Thanks, Maggie," Rose said, heading for the door.

"See you soon," she called after them.

They stepped out into the heat, and Bodhi saw that Rose had placed the bags of groceries in the bed of the truck. He put the table in on its side and then wedged the rug on the seat with the lamp and books. The truck was hot, and by the time he was done, sweat was trickling down his back.

He met Rose's eye over the hood. "Any ice cream in this town?"

He saw something wary drop over her eyes. "We have ice cream."

"Well, we can't get in this truck until we have ice cream," he said. "My treat."

She hesitated, like she might refuse. A few seconds later she sighed, like she was giving in after some kind of long argument.

"I actually think I might agree."

He smiled and shut the door.

They walked across the street to a little stand on the corner that served ice cream and other fast food. Bodhi took his time with the menu before deciding on a double scoop of chocolate chip cookie dough. When it was Rose's turn, she ordered a scoop of raspberry sorbet and one of chocolate ice cream without looking at the menu.

"Come here often?" Bodhi asked her with a smile.

She nodded. "The Breiners supply this place with milk and cream."

"I bet it's good," Bodhi said while they waited for their cones.

"It is."

They sat at one of the old picnic tables on a deck at the back of the ice cream stand. It looked out on a sparse group of trees fronting a small river. He tried to focus on the water instead of Rose. Her hair was in its usual braid, and Bodhi couldn't help wondering what it would look like loose, if the sun would light it on fire.

"What?" Rose said.

He'd been staring. "Nothing."

She smiled a little. "Nothing?"

"I . . . well." He cleared his throat a little. "I like your hair."

Her smile got a little bit bigger before it faded. "Thank you." She licked around the outside of her cone where the raspberry was melting into the chocolate.

They were still sitting there in silence when Will Breiner came around the corner.

"I thought that was you," he said to Rose. "Going for ice cream without me?"

Was there a note of accusation in his voice, like Rose wasn't allowed to have ice cream with anyone but him? Bodhi had to tamp down a rush of something too close to jealousy to be called anything else. He didn't own Rose.

Then again, neither did Will Breiner.

Rose laughed. "It was a last minute thing. I had some errands to run and so did Bodhi, so . . ."

Will nodded.

"Why don't you join us?" Rose offered.

He looked at her dripping cone and then at Bodhi. "Looks like you're almost done."

"We can wait," she said.

Will seemed to think about it before shaking his head. "Next time. Besides, you know we'll be here all summer when it's too hot to sleep."

Another meaningful glance at Bodhi.

Rose smiled. Was she unaware of Will's posturing? Or was she just being diplomatic by not acknowledging it?

"How's that bull?" Will asked suddenly.

Rose turned to Bodhi. "I forgot to ask. Have you had any trouble getting him in and out?"

Bodhi shook his head. "Not a one."

Will almost looked disappointed. "Glad to hear it." He gave them a tight smile. "I have to make some more deliveries, but I'll see you around, Rose. Maybe go for a swim later?"

She nodded.

Will looked at Bodhi. "See you around."

Bodhi smiled. "Without a doubt."

He turned his eyes back to the water, swallowing his annoyance. He didn't have a right to be annoyed. He was the one who didn't belong here, not Will.

Twenty-One

"Still a bit small," Bodhi said, chewing on a piece of hay while he watched Buttercup.

"I'm working on it," Rose said.

They were standing at the fence in the back field, watching the cows graze. Bodhi had been on the farm for a couple of weeks, but Rose had turned down his offers to help with Buttercup. The calf felt like her responsibility, even though she couldn't explain why. Sometimes when Rose was trying to bottle-feed her, Bodhi would open his mouth like he was going to say something, then close it real fast like he'd changed his mind. But Rose knew the calf wasn't doing well. She saw it in the way the animal refused to run, and in her eyes and mouth, both of which were drier than they should have been. She saw it in Buttercup's lethargy, in the way she watched listlessly as the other calves romped around the field.

Rose was being stubborn and she knew it, but the farm was the one place where she felt like the ground was solid under her feet. She may not know what to do about her dad, may not have any idea what her future held, but she could manage the farm. Okay, she needed help with the day-to-day stuff, but she knew what she was doing, and part of her was clinging to that knowledge with everything she had, because if she didn't know what she was doing here, what else was there for her?

She looked at Bodhi in her peripheral vision, surprised to realize they hadn't spoken for the past few minutes. Somewhere along the way, their silences had gotten less uncomfortable, probably because she was getting used to their routine, which was leisurely compared to what she'd been dealing with on her own. Bodhi took care of the animals in the morning, allowing her two glorious extra hours of sleep. She joined him once the sun was up, and they cleaned out the barn before breakfast. After that, Bodhi spent the morning and early afternoon seeing to maintenance on the fences, irrigation systems, and outbuildings while Rose took care of the kitchen garden, did any paperwork that was required to keep the farm running, and checked on her dad. She still ate lunch alone, although she'd gotten used to bumping into Bodhi in the kitchen while they made something to eat in the middle of the day. After lunch, Rose walked over to the Breiners' farm to say hello or went swimming. Sometimes she'd be lying on the bank of the pond, the sun warming her face, when she would sit up, suddenly sure there was something she should be doing, some chore on the farm that must need tending. But then she'd remember: Bodhi was there. He had everything under control, and she alternated between being relieved and annoyed that she was coming to rely on him.

She didn't know what he did in the afternoons. She imagined him up in the hayloft, the smell of burned wood and hay scenting the air as he read one of the books she saw him carrying around. That had surprised her, that he liked to read. She wasn't sure why. She knew that farming and intelligence weren't mutually exclusive. But he hadn't seemed the type, and the first time she'd seen him reading at the kitchen table, she'd felt almost embarrassed, like she'd caught him in the middle of something personal.

"Could do with some rain," Bodhi said next to her, shaking her from her thoughts.

She nodded. "Could."

They stood there a few more minutes before she heard the sound of gravel crunching behind them. She turned to see Marty approaching, looking half her age in jeans and a T-shirt, her hair loose around her shoulders.

"Hey!" She smiled as she kissed Rose on the cheek. "How's my favorite niece?"

Rose laughed. "I'd be flattered if I wasn't your only niece."

Marty waved away her comment. "Details!" She looked at Bodhi. "How's it going, Bodhi?"

He nodded. "Getting the lay of the land."

"Glad to hear it," Marty said. Her gaze scanned the field and rested on Buttercup. "Is that the little calf you birthed in the spring?"

Rose nodded.

"Is she sick?" Marty asked. "She looks small."

"She's not feeding as well as I'd like," Rose said. "But I'm working on it."

"Did you tell your dad?" Marty asked.

"Not yet."

Marty's expression grew thoughtful. "You might need to get Doc Russell in here."

Rose swallowed the lump in her throat. "I will if she doesn't get better. I'm going to give it another week."

"Don't wait too long," Marty said.

Rose nodded. "What are you doing here?" she asked, anxious to change the subject.

"I had to journey to civilization to pick up a few things."

Bodhi looked confused. "Civilization?"

"Poughkeepsie," Rose explained. "And honestly, I'm surprised she even counts that as civilization. She's lowered the bar since she first came back from Thailand."

Marty grinned. "Desperate times call for desperate measures. Poughkeepsie is as close to civilization as I'm going to get without going into the city." She looked at Rose. "I stopped at that market you like and picked up a few things. Want to come see?"

"Definitely," Rose said. "Did you get those chocolate-covered cherries? Lexie's staying tonight. She loves those."

Marty draped a slender arm across Rose's shoulders. "Only one way to find out."

Marty lifted one hand in the air as they turned to the house. "Bye, Bodhi."

"See you, Marty."

"So?" Marty asked Rose as they stepped into the house. "How's it going?"

"With Bodhi?" Rose asked.

"Yes, with Bodhi." Her aunt laughed. "Is he working out okay?"

Rose bit her lip. "It's a big help, having him here."

"Why do you make that sound like a bad thing?" Marty asked.

Rose followed Marty into the kitchen. "I don't know. I don't mean to."

She leaned against the counter while Marty started taking things out of the paper bags lined up there. She handed Rose two plastic containers of chocolate-covered cherries on her way to the fridge.

"Thank you!" Rose said. "I'll hide one of these before Lexie gets here."

But Marty was frozen in front of the fridge.

"What's wrong?" Rose asked.

Marty looked at her. "I should be asking you that question. There's no food in here. What on earth are you guys eating?"

"What?" Rose walked to the fridge and stood next to her aunt. "There's food! Tons of food!"

Marty shut the door of the fridge and crossed her arms over her chest. "Premade casseroles, orange juice, and condiments don't count as food."

"I need to go to the store, that's all. I went last week. I just haven't had a chance to go back." Rose crossed to the paper bags and removed a container of goat cheese and a package of French bread.

Marty spoke quietly behind her. "Tell me you've been making meals for him, Rose."

Rose tried to laugh to lighten the mood. "I don't need to cook for him! He's an adult. He makes his own food, and I make mine. It's working out fine."

Marty rubbed her forehead like she had a sudden headache. "It's not fine, Rose. It's part of the deal that we make him feel at home here. That includes making meals. You know as well as I do that farming is hard work. You can't expect him to live on casseroles cooked four months ago, not with all the labor he's doing here."

"He can make something for himself if he's still hungry," Rose said, but she hated herself even as she said it. Hated how careless and selfish she sounded. Bodhi was lightening her load so she could rest and swim, and she hadn't even made him a meal.

"You know how to cook," Marty said softly. "You even *like* cooking."

"Not anymore," Rose muttered before she could stop herself.

Silence filled the kitchen in the moment before Marty spoke again. "I know it's something you did with your mom. Cooking, baking . . . You spent a lot of your time together in here. I understand how it might be hard for you to do it without her."

Rose felt tears sting her eyes and had to resist the urge to cover her ears. She didn't want to talk about this with Marty. She was okay as long as she didn't think about it too hard. As long as she didn't *remember*. Because remembering—the sound of her mother's voice, the feel of her mother's hand on hers when she was teaching Rose to knead bread dough, the smell of her peach pie in the oven—that just hurt too much.

Rose crossed her arms and leaned against the counter. "I'm fine. I'm just busy."

Marty's eyes flashed. "That may be true, but so is Bodhi. And you will make him feel at home here. Have you even thought how it must be for him? Far from home without a single friend? Working all day and then heating up old casseroles in the microwave? You probably make him eat alone, too."

Rose felt her cheeks grow hot.

"Oh, Rose . . ." Disappointment and sadness mingled in her aunt's voice.

Rose couldn't stand it. "Stop feeling bad for me! I'm *fine*. Bodhi is fine. It's not like he's complaining."

"Well, I am. I'm complaining, okay? And if your mother were here, she'd be complaining, too. She would never allow you to be this inhospitable. You know it's true. Bodhi is here to take care of the farm. You are to make things easier for him while he does." Marty's voice had turned steely, and Rose knew there was no point arguing. "Are we clear?"

"As a bell," Rose muttered.

"Good." She hesitated, then walked over to Rose and

pulled her into an embrace. "I love you, honey. I know you're hurting. I'm hurting, too. But when I look at you, I see her, and suddenly everything's okay." She kissed the top of Rose's head. "I have to go, but I'll check in on you soon. Enjoy your sleepover with Lexie."

Rose listened to Marty's footsteps recede down the hall. She didn't start crying until after she heard the screen door slam, and she stood there for a minute, swiping at the hot tears on her cheeks, remembering Marty's words.

But when I look at you, I see her, and suddenly everything's okay.

If only it were that simple.

Twenty-Two

"I know you have another container of these somewhere." Lexie popped a chocolate-covered cherry in her mouth and flipped the page of the magazine spread out in front of her.

Rose was sitting at her desk, scrolling through her playlists. "I don't! Marty only brought me one."

"Liar." Lexie grinned, then pointed to the page she was reading. "You should do this. You can totally pull this off."

"What?" Rose leaned in to look.

"This boho rocker thing. It's really coming back." She seemed to think about it. "Well, technically it started a couple of years ago, but now it's becoming more mainstream."

"Do I look like a boho rocker to you?" Rose asked.

Lexie looked up at her, and Rose could see that she was taking the question seriously. "Yeah, you do, actually." She got up and went to Rose's closet. "And you can do it with stuff you have. Like this." She pulled out a dress covered in sunflowers and threw it on the bed. She studied Rose for a few seconds. "You just need to leave your hair down more often, maybe wear some sandals or boots."

"I wear boots all the time!" Rose protested. "You always complain when I wear them!"

"Let me clarify; I should have said, 'Boots without cow poop on them.'"

"I don't have anything like that," Rose said.

"Which is exactly the problem. We are so going thrift shopping in the city in the fall."

Rose started one of her playlists, and the room filled with the sound of chords strummed softly from an acoustic guitar. "If you say so."

"I'm going to get some milk," Lexie said. "Want anything?"

Rose shook her head. "I'm good."

Lexie disappeared into the hall, and Rose stood, crossing the room to the sundress on the bed. Her mother had bought it for her at the Brooklyn Flea from a woman who made dresses out of vintage patterns. She'd already purchased a big floppy hat with a sunflower on it for herself earlier in the day.

"Look! We'll match!" she had exclaimed when she saw the dress.

It was late September, and the sun had already started to take on the glow unique to autumn. Rose had worn the dress exactly once before her mom had gotten sick.

"Hi, honey."

The voice startled her, and she spun around, surprised to

see her dad standing in the doorway. He was wearing jeans and a flannel shirt, as if he'd been out with the herd, repairing fences and irrigation ditches with Bodhi when he'd been in the house all day instead.

"Hi, Daddy."

"You and Lexie having a nice time?"

She saw something in his eyes. A hint of desperation. He was trying, going through the motions of being her dad, and even this simple thing was hard for him. She felt a sudden swell of anger. Her mother was dead. Why couldn't he just deal with it? It's what she had to do. Why couldn't he make things easier, make things *normal*, for her?

"Yep." She immediately regretted the tone in her voice. She took a deep breath. "Everything's good, Dad. What are you up to?"

"Oh, not much. Watching a movie on cable."

Rose tried to smile. "Oh yeah? Which one?"

"The Quiet Man."

"John Wayne," Rose said softly.

He looked surprised. "How did you know?"

"We watched it one summer," she reminded him. "You and me and mom."

His eyes glazed over, and she knew he was trying to remember. "Did we?"

She nodded. "Mom made popcorn, but she left the lid off the pan and it went all over the kitchen."

"That's right. We were still finding popcorn at Christmas."

Was she imagining that the corners of his mouth turned up a little?

"It's a good movie," she said.

He nodded.

"Oh, hi, Mr. Darrow!" Lexie turned sideways and slipped into the room around Rose's dad.

"Hello, Lexie," he said. "How have you been?"

"Oh, you know, Mr. Darrow, better than nothing."

Rose rolled her eyes. She recognized a Grandma Russell quote when she heard one.

"Glad to hear it." He seemed to hesitate. "Well, I'll leave you girls to it."

"Bye, Dad."

"Bye, Mr. Darrow."

Rose heard his footsteps retreat down the hall, then the soft click of his bedroom door. She wouldn't see him again until tomorrow.

Lexie pointed accusingly at her. "I knew it!"

"What are you talking about?"

She crossed her arms over her chest. "He *is* hot!"

It took Rose a minute to shift gears. "Wait . . . are you talking about Bodhi?"

"Oh, I am definitely talking about Bodhi," Lexie said, pulling Rose down onto the bed next to her. "And you're going to be talking about him, too. You owe me."

Rose laughed. "I have no idea what you mean."

"Please," Lexie said, "don't tell me you haven't noticed how smoking that guy is. Not to mention young! When you said he was a little older I was thinking midtwenties. What is he, nineteen? Twenty?"

Rose walked to her computer, turning her face to the

screen and scrolling through the songs on her playlist to avoid Lexie's scrutiny. "Somewhere around there, I think."

"So?" Lexie was on the verge of squealing with excitement.

Rose turned around. "So, what? And how do you even know what he looks like?"

"I was in the kitchen, just minding my own business, when in walks this tall drink of water, and—"

"A tall drink of water?" Rose interrupted. "Does anyone say that anymore?"

Lexie looked offended. "I don't care if anyone says it or not. They *should*, that's the point." She scowled at Rose before continuing. "Anyway, in walks this super hunk of a guy, and he says, with his big, deep man voice, 'Hello, I'm Bodhi Lowell.'"

"And?" Rose said.

"And! Broad shoulders? Muscly thighs? Abs you can slice bread on?"

"Abs you can . . ." Rose narrowed her eyes. "How do you know he has good abs?"

Lexie shrugged. "He had his shirt off." She grinned. "But you totally said that like you've noticed his abs. Nice, right?"

Rose turned back to her computer. "I did not notice his abs. I was just surprised you did, that's all."

"Uh-huh," Lexie said behind her. Rose could hear the smile in her voice even if she couldn't see it. "Has anyone ever told you that you're a terrible liar?"

Rose didn't answer, just tried to focus on the songs scrolling through her feed while she tried *not* to think about

Bodhi Lowell's abs. For a minute, Lexie didn't say anything, and Rose thought maybe she'd dropped it.

"It's okay to be happy, you know." Lexie's voice was soft, and Rose turned to face her.

"I know that," Rose said. "I'm just not."

"But you could be," Lexie said. "And you could start by taking advantage of the fact that you have a hot, interesting guy living with you for the summer—one who isn't from Milford."

Rose swallowed against the emotion that rose in her throat. How could she tell Lexie that getting close to Bodhi was dangerous? That keeping up a pretense of normalcy while he lived in the bunkhouse was only possible because she never let him see the truth? She'd never been in a serious relationship before, but she was pretty sure it meant letting the other person in, letting them see the real you.

And what was the point in that? You let people in, got attached to them, and they left anyway, one way or another. Even Lexie would be leaving. It's just how life was. Bodhi Lowell would move on at the end of the summer. She'd never see him again, and it would be just one more hole to fill.

Right now, she could live with the thought. She hardly knew him, and as long as she kept it that way, she would be just fine.

Twenty-Three

The heat of the day was just starting to seep into the hayloft when Bodhi took off his shirt and sat down at his computer. He'd seen Rose in the kitchen at lunch and was trying to ignore the clock in his head, counting down the hours until he'd see her again. He told himself it was normal. He'd been on the Darrow farm for over two weeks, and Rose was the only company he had other than the few times he'd been into town.

He wasn't entirely sure he believed it.

He wasn't even sure what it was about her that intrigued him. Sometimes he thought it was her silence, the way she could work next to him for hours without saying two words and without expecting him to talk either. But then she'd make some offhand comment, an observation about the farm, or even more rare, about life, and he'd realize that she was smart and strong, and he liked those things about her, too.

He had a flash of her then, her hair wet and loose down

her back when she came back from the pond, the sun striking it gold and copper and amber all at the same time. She had a strong set to her shoulders, even when she didn't think anyone was looking, like she was carrying the whole farm on her back and could keep on doing it forever. The fact that she shouldn't have to was a subject he hadn't figured out how to broach. Her dad probably needed professional help, and Marty had done what she could for Rose by way of hiring Bodhi. Will was there when Rose really needed something, but while Bodhi could tell that Will cared about her, he could see that Will wanted something from her, too, even if she couldn't see it yet. Bodhi didn't like the idea of someone wanting something from Rose. He had a feeling she was barely standing as it was.

He logged into his email, grateful the barn had Wi-Fi for the office, and tried to put Rose out of his mind. She wasn't his problem. He would help while he was here. That was the best he could do. He had problems of his own.

His inbox opened in front of him and he started clearing it out by deleting all the obvious junk mail. He was about halfway down the page when he saw a familiar address, CBurton4298@gmail.com.

His gut clenched a little as he opened the message.

Hey, Bodhi. How's it going? Wanted to see if you've heard from your dad. Saw him a couple weeks back and he wasn't in good shape. Mentioned trying to find you. Haven't seen him since. Any sign of him on your end?
Christine

He sat back in the chair, the words swimming on the screen in front of him. Christine Burton had been one of his dad's many girlfriends back when Bodhi was a kid. Bodhi hadn't remembered much about her—white-blond hair, a tattoo of the infinity symbol on her wrist, a husky laugh—until he'd run into her a couple years back when he was working a ranch outside of Billings. He hadn't recognized her at first, but she'd recognized him, and they'd spent an hour over lunch catching up. It was the first contact he'd had with someone who knew his dad since he'd left home. He didn't know what he expected. To hear that his dad had sobered up? That he missed Bodhi and had been looking for him?

The news he got was a lot more predictable: his dad in debt up to his eyeballs to the wrong people, still drinking. He could tell that Christine was sorry for the whole mess, and they'd kept in touch via email ever since, even if it was only once a year or so.

Now his mind strayed back into dangerous territory. His dad was looking for him. Maybe he *had* cleaned up. Maybe he wanted to apologize. To make things right with his only kid.

Bodhi shook his head in the empty room. No sense going down that road. His dad was behind him. He typed a quick message to Christine.

No word on my end, but I'm in New York now. Hope you're doing well.
Bodhi

He closed his computer and tried to think about something else. After lunch, he'd spent some time with the little calf Rose liked, just watching her, trying to get a handle on her failure to thrive. He'd seen the worry in Rose's eyes when they'd talked about the calf a few days ago, but he also sensed something desperate and personal about Rose's bid to take care of the animal. He suspected it had something to do with the green fly tag in Buttercup's ear. Green had been her mother's favorite color, Rose had told him, and it was the way they marked the calves bred by Kate Darrow before her death.

Over the past two weeks, he'd watched Rose bottle-feed the animal, watched her bawl and pull away, kicking and making a fuss until Rose was so frustrated she'd stomped from the barn, her cheeks flaming with frustration. Bodhi thought there might be a better way to approach the problem, but he didn't want to step on Rose's toes. On the other hand, he didn't want the little calf to die, and he knew Rose didn't want her dad selling Buttercup either. Not yet.

He got up and lay on his bed, cracking open his most recent acquisition from the library in town. It was an old book called *Shane*, about a ranch hand who gets involved in a homesteading war in 1800s Wyoming. It was probably corny, but he'd added it to his pile on the way to the front desk anyway. He tried to read, but he was still thinking about Buttercup, trying to find a way to help her and ignoring the voice in his head that said it wasn't Buttercup he was worried about at all.

Twenty-Four

"Come on!" Rose said through gritted teeth. "Why are you backing away from me? You're going to starve to death!"

Rose had led Buttercup inside one of the horse stalls in the little barn, hoping to eliminate the distraction of the other cows. Bodhi watched from outside the stall as the calf backed away, then trotted to the corner and faced away from Rose like she wanted to pretend Rose wasn't there.

"Ugh!" Rose swiped at a piece of hair that had come loose from her braid. "How am I supposed to get you to eat if I can't even keep you in one place?"

It was a rhetorical question, but Bodhi sensed an opening. "I might have an idea."

She looked up at him with surprise, like she'd forgotten he was there. "Well, good, because I'm fresh out."

He gestured to the stall. "Mind?"

"Be my guest."

He grabbed a rope off one of the hooks outside the stall, stepped inside, and closed the door behind him.

"I've already tried the rope," Rose said. "It keeps her from running around but she still thrashes, so I can't even get the bottle close to her mouth."

He held out a hand and she gave him the bottle, although for a second he thought he'd have to pry it from her hands. Then he strode across the barn to the corner where Buttercup still faced the wall. She sensed him coming and tried to back up, but he was already too close, and he looped the rope around her head and threw one leg over her back. The animal tried to buck, but Bodhi put a little of his weight on Buttercup's back and clenched his thighs around the calf's midsection to immobilize her.

"Come here," he said.

"Me?" Rose asked.

"Yep." She walked tentatively toward him and he gestured to the space he'd left in front of him on Buttercup's back. "Sit."

"What . . . there?"

"Yep."

"There's . . . there's not enough room," she said.

He glanced up at her face and was surprised to see that her cheeks were flushed. "There's plenty of room. Now come on. If you want to learn, you need to do it, not watch me do it."

She stepped closer and swung a leg over the animal's

back. She was nestled in front of him now, her back nearly flush with his torso. He reached around her with one arm to give her the bottle.

"Take this." She did, and he put his own hand around her smaller one. His arms were snug against her shoulders. "Now you have to be forceful. Keep her still with your thighs. You have to squeeze. Show her who's boss."

A current of electricity rushed through his body as he felt her tighten her thighs in front of his.

"Now use your other hand to pry open her mouth," Bodhi instructed. "It's not a request, so don't make it seem like one."

She struggled in front of him, fumbling with the bottle while Buttercup tried in vain to get away. Bodhi helped by keeping his thighs tight against the calf and squeezing if she ever got too frisky. He used one hand to help Rose hold the calf's mouth open, and a minute later, he heard the sounds of suckling, felt the gentle tug at the other end of his hand.

"I think she's doing it!" Rose turned around, her face flushed and only inches from his. They both froze, and everything else seemed to fall away. All he could see was her face. He realized now that her eyes weren't just green. They were the color of a river, clean and clear, that he'd fished in Wyoming. He could hear it rushing as he looked at her, could remember standing on the bank, watching the light throw a thousand diamonds into the water.

"I think you're right." Bodhi's voice was hoarse, and he

cleared his throat as he stepped off the calf. "Let me take a look."

He eased around to the front of the calf, and sure enough, there she was, suckling at the bottle like she'd known how to do it all along. He studied the animal for a minute, trying to get his heartbeat under control, to calm the rush of feeling that had made him want to kiss Rose Darrow when that was the very last thing he needed.

"I think she's got it," Bodhi said, finally daring to meet Rose's eyes.

A smile broke across her face, like the sun letting loose its first ray of light across the fields in the morning. "Really?"

He nodded, swallowing the lump that had risen in his throat. It was the first time she'd really smiled—without hesitation or sadness or suspicion—in front of him. It was a smile that broke his heart and made it whole again all at the same time.

Later, after they'd put Buttercup back in with the other cows, they walked to the front of the barn together.

"Will she be okay now?" Rose asked.

Bodhi thought about the question. He didn't want to lie, but he also didn't want to be responsible for killing the light he'd seen in her eyes back in the barn.

"There's never any guarantee. If she's had trouble being consistent in the past, there's always the possibility she'll find a way around this new system. But I think she's got a good shot. And at least now you know how to keep her still."

Her cheeks flushed pink, like she was remembering their

proximity in the barn. He knew he wouldn't forget it anytime soon.

She looked into his eyes. "Thank you. I'm sorry I was . . ."

"Bullheaded?" he offered.

She laughed. "Yeah, okay. I'm sorry I was bullheaded. It kind of runs in my family."

"There are worse things," Bodhi said. "Sometimes being bullheaded is the only thing that's kept me upright."

He regretted the words as soon as he said them. The last thing he needed was for Rose to know his life story. If she didn't think he was a loser now, she would then. But it was too late; he saw the shadow of interest, and maybe even something like surprise.

"Anyway," he continued before she could seize on the opportunity to ask him any questions. "I'm glad it worked out. Maybe I'll see you in the house for dinner?"

She seemed to think about it before nodding. "Maybe."

He turned and headed back into the barn, climbed the ladder to the hayloft, and fell onto his bed, his heart thumping a mile a minute.

Not good.

Twenty-Five

Rose was throwing bug spray and water into her bag on the Fourth of July when she heard a knock at the front door. She hurried down the stairs to find Bodhi standing on the other side of the screen door.

"You don't have to knock," she said, opening the door. "Just come in."

She took in his well-worn jeans and black T-shirt as he stepped inside. Jeans and T-shirts were his uniform, but she was still sometimes surprised by how good he looked in them.

"You sure you don't need me to bring anything?" he asked.

Rose shook her head. "I think I've got it, although I'm planning to fill up on funnel cake so I didn't pack any actual food."

He laughed a little. "Sounds like a plan."

Going to the town's Fourth of July carnival hadn't been her idea. Lexie was in the city scoping out the apartment she'd be sharing with three other girls in the fall, and Will had an emergency with a lactating cow. Rose figured she'd just stay home and try to see the fireworks from there. But then Marty had stopped by, begging Rose to go with her. It was only after Rose agreed to go that Marty invited Bodhi.

Rose didn't know if it was because she was getting used to having him around or because she was still replaying their closeness in the barn, but the idea of eating carnival food, riding the Ferris wheel, and playing games with Bodhi somehow didn't seem half bad. Plus, Marty would be there to keep it from getting too awkward.

Her phone buzzed with a text from Lexie.

Have fun with the studmuffin.

Rose sighed and texted her back.

Don't get excited. It's purely platonic.

Rose turned to Bodhi. "You ready?"

"Aren't we waiting for Marty?" he asked.

"She's going to meet us there," Rose said.

"Then I'm good to go."

"Great." She reached for her bag, but Bodhi got there before her.

"I can get that," she said.

"It's no problem."

She got the feeling that it was some kind of old-school chivalry, which meant she didn't stand a chance of changing his mind, so she grabbed her keys and headed for the door. Her phone buzzed as she was stepping onto the porch.

For now. ;)

Rose sighed.

"Something wrong?" Bodhi asked.

"No. Lexie's just a pain sometimes."

He chuckled. "She does seem like a handful."

"That's one word for it."

They got in the truck and headed for the carnival. Cars were backed up around the firehouse, and it took them a good twenty minutes to follow the waving arms of the officers working traffic control to a spot on the grass.

They started for the carnival site, the Ferris wheel rising into the sky as other rides dipped and whirled, their lights on even though it wasn't quite dark. The smell of fried dough and lemonade drifted to her on the dust—they still hadn't had any rain—and the lighthearted screams of people on the rides got louder as they approached the fair.

"What do you want to ride first?" The words were out of her mouth before she could stop them.

He laughed. "Someone's excited."

She couldn't help smiling. "Just a little."

"What about Marty?"

"I say we buy tickets and take one ride. You snooze you lose, and Marty is snoozing."

He grinned. "I'm in."

They bought tickets at the booth and got in line for the Vortex, then spent five minutes smashed against the side of the ride while it got faster and faster. She was still breathing heavily when they emerged from the exit side of the ride.

"That was crazy!" she said. "Didn't you think we were going to fly out when they lifted up those walls on the inside?"

"Nah," he said.

She rolled her eyes. "What? You're too cool to be scared?"

"Okay, I was a little scared," he admitted.

"I knew it!"

They made their way back to the entrance, but Marty still wasn't there.

"Where is she?" Rose pulled out her phone. "I'm going to call her."

But she already had a text message from Marty, and it wasn't one saying she was on her way.

"I should have known," she muttered.

"What?" Bodhi asked.

She held up her phone so he could read the text: **Deadline pushed forward on Amsterdam article. Can't make it. Have fun without me!**

Bodhi looked at her. "Do you want to go home?"

She sighed. She didn't want to go home. But she also didn't want to be some kind of matchmaking experience for her aunt.

"No. We're here," Rose said. "We might as well have fun." She hesitated. "Unless . . . do you want to go home?"

"No way," he said. "You promised me funnel cake."

She laughed. "Lexie would say we're in for a penny, in for a pound."

"So would half the old ladies I've ever known," Bodhi said.

"Exactly."

They bought more tickets and made their way from ride to ride, starting with the Ferris wheel and ending up back at the Vortex. They played Duck Hunt (Bodhi won her a giant stuffed duck) and tried to get ping-pong balls into cups of water (she won Bodhi a goldfish, but he only agreed to accept it if they could set it loose in the pond). In between they ate hot dogs, two funnel cakes apiece, and cotton candy that turned their tongues blue.

"I think I feel sick," Rose said as they made their way to the big open field to watch fireworks.

Bodhi laughed. "You did it to yourself."

"Hey!" She punched him playfully on the arm. "You ate as much as me!"

"Yeah, but I'm not complaining about it." He surveyed the field, dotted with blankets and picnic baskets as people settled in for the fireworks. "Any idea where you want to sit?"

"I usually sit over there." She pointed to the right, far enough outside a bank of trees that they could still see the fireworks, but at the edge of the crowd.

"Looks good." He headed that way, carrying the bag Rose had packed even though she must have told him a hundred times that she could carry it.

Rose knew just about everybody in Milford, and they all wanted to see how she was doing as she and Bodhi picked their way through the crowd. For the first time in a long time, it didn't bother her. It felt good to be part of something, to know there were people out there who wanted her to be okay. She introduced Bodhi to Marie and her daughter, Clementine, and was surprised to realize Bodhi already knew Mrs. Rand, the town librarian. They stopped to talk to Allison, the woman who owned the flower shop in town, and again to speak to Maggie Ryland.

When they finally got to the spot near the trees, Bodhi reached into the bag and took out the blanket Rose had packed, then spread it out on the ground so they could sit. Rose removed two water bottles and handed one to Bodhi.

"This is a nice spot," he said, looking around. "Will the fireworks be over there?" He pointed to the clearing left of the trees.

"Yep. You'll get a perfect view, I promise."

"Well, good. Because you do not want to see me when I haven't had my Fourth of July fireworks."

He said it with such a straight face that it took her a few seconds to realize he was kidding.

"No wonder you and Marty get along," Rose said. "To hear her tell it, she just couldn't go on if she missed the fireworks. And now she's not even here."

"Am I wrong to smell a setup?" Bodhi asked.

"Not wrong at all."

He sighed, and she thought she heard a smile in it. "I see."

She turned her head to look at him. "Sorry."

He met her gaze. "It's not so bad."

Time seemed to stretch and thin, almost to stop as she looked into his eyes. Then the lights in the field went out and the music started, followed by the first of the fireworks. She kept her head tilted to the sky, but her mind was on Bodhi. On the way he looked and the way it felt to have his long legs stretched out next to hers, their shoulders only inches apart as light exploded in the sky over their heads.

Twenty-Six

"Isn't it weird to think we don't have to go back to school?" Will spoke from beside her on the bank of the pond.

It had been two days since Bodhi had showed Rose how to restrain and feed Buttercup. Two days during which she'd thought about Bodhi almost every waking minute, remembering the feel of him behind her on the calf, his arms wrapped around her, the only two minutes in the last ten months that she'd felt really safe. She forced herself to focus on the feel of the sun on her body, the sound of Will breathing next to her.

"Speak for yourself," she finally said.

"I'll go to community college eventually, too," he said. "There's no rush. It's not like it's going anywhere."

"True." She said it, but she couldn't imagine it. Bad

enough to stay in Milford doing the same thing day after day, seeing the same people (not that she didn't love them). At least going to school meant there would be something more to her life. Something to learn. New people to meet.

"When does Bodhi leave?" Will asked.

Rose laughed, her eyes still closed. "He just got here." She sat up, shading her eyes from the sun as she looked at Will, stretched out on the bank of the pond in his swim trunks. "You don't like him very much, do you?"

He plucked at the wild grass near his leg. "Don't know him."

"It doesn't seem like you want to either," she said.

He shrugged. "He just seems a little . . . comfortable, that's all."

"Is he supposed to be uncomfortable?" Rose asked. "I mean, this is his home for the summer. I want him to be comfortable."

Will's head snapped up, his eyes meeting hers. "Do you like him?"

She looked away, busied herself with lip balm to avoid Will's eyes. "I don't know him either. Not really. But I like him well enough."

"Do you guys . . . you know, spend time together?" he asked. "Like, hanging out when you're not working the farm?"

She heard the too-casual note in his voice and knew he was fishing. She looked at her phone, hunting for an excuse to leave. She didn't want to talk about Bodhi with Will.

"I have to get back," she said. "It's almost time to bring in the herd."

"Isn't that what Bodhi's here for?" Will asked.

The challenge in his voice annoyed her. Why was he suddenly questioning her about Bodhi? Being friends didn't give him a right to stick his nose in her business.

"I don't just sit around watching *Oprah* all day because we have one person helping out on the farm." Rose caught the annoyance in her voice and tried to soften her tone. Will was more than a friend. He was like a brother. "You know how it is, Will. It's not like you don't have to work just because you have hired help."

He stood, sighing. "I'm sorry." He looked into her eyes. "I don't want you to get hurt."

"I don't know what you're talking about." She bent to pick up her towel.

When she stood, he placed a hand on her arm. "He's going to leave, Rose."

She smiled. She was going for carefree, but it didn't feel that way on her face. "I know that."

"Just . . . don't get attached, okay? You've had a rough few months."

She was suddenly angry at him. Angry for reminding her of a loss she could never forget anyway. Of making it seem like she wasn't even entitled to this one moment of possibility. Even if he was right—and she knew he was—it felt crappy.

"Nothing's going on, Will. He's hired help. Period." She

looped the towel around her neck. "I have to get back. See you later."

"Text me," he said to her back.

She didn't answer, just kept walking, a mixture of anger and loss winding itself through her body like a summer storm. She hurried through the orchard, anxious to get back and change so she could saddle Raven in time to herd with Bodhi. She'd come to enjoy it, the moments they rode side by side on horseback. Sometime in the last couple of weeks, their silences had become comfortable, the tension between them mellowing into something that felt almost like familiarity.

It was nice to have his company. Nicer than she wanted to admit.

She caught sight of her dad in the garage on the way to the house and raised an arm in greeting. He raised one back, and for a split second, she felt like everything was okay. That's how her grief had started to feel; if she looked at it from a distance, it was a little out of focus, almost manageable. It was only when she came too close to it that she remembered how bad it was.

Pulling open the screen door, she dropped her stuff on the bench in the foyer and clattered up the stairs to her room. She took off her damp suit so she wouldn't have wet marks under her T-shirt, then pulled on her cutoffs and ran back down the stairs.

She'd made good time, and she decided to take a quick look at Buttercup before saddling Raven. They were rotating the herd to keep the fields fertile, and today the cattle were in the small field between the two barns. She stood at the fence, scanning the animals for Buttercup. She saw the other babies playing in one corner of the pasture while the adults looked on, but she didn't see Buttercup, not at first.

Finally, she spotted the calf against the fence at the far side of the field. Why was she lying there? It was true that she hadn't fed as well since the day in the barn with Bodhi, but Rose was sure she was getting some milk into the animal.

She hopped the fence and strode toward Buttercup. The other animals started bawling at her, moving in closer, thinking she was going to feed them. She fake lunged at them and said, "Get!" to make them go away. Then she turned her attention back to Buttercup.

The calf was lying with her back up against the fence, kicking at her belly. Rose could tell even from where she stood that Buttercup's stomach was round and hard. It only took her a second to turn and start running.

She raced across the field, scrabbled over the fence, then ran full speed into the barn.

"Bodhi!" she called out. "Are you in here?"

His head appeared at the top of the hayloft.

"Rose! What's wrong?" He was already on his way down the ladder. "Is everything okay?"

"It's Buttercup," Rose panted. "I think she has bloat."

Twenty-Seven

They used a small motorized cart to bring Buttercup into the barn. Fear rang through Rose's body when she got up close to the animal. She was listless, her eyes glassy. Bloat was no joke. It was deadly, particularly to calves, and Buttercup's condition was bad.

Bodhi steered the golf cart to the horse barn while Rose sat in the back with Buttercup, trying to brace the calf against the bumps and ruts in the field. She knew why Bodhi wasn't heading for the cattle barn; the galleys, long and open, offered little private space to nurse an injured animal.

When they got to the barn, Bodhi stopped just outside the doors and hurried inside. He returned a minute later with one of the wheeled trolleys they used to move dirt and small amounts of hay.

"Let's get her in here," Bodhi said, parking the trolley

right up against the back of the motorized cart. He grabbed the calf's hind legs while Rose took the front, and they half slid, half lifted Buttercup into the trolley. "Nice and easy."

The fact that she made it easy for them only made Rose worry more. A healthy calf would fight them.

"Let's get her inside." Bodhi grabbed ahold of the trolley's handle and started pulling while Rose spoke softly to Buttercup, trying to soothe her in case she was scared.

They passed the stall holding Coco, and Rose thought she saw something sad and knowing in the animal's eyes. She heard her mother's voice, murmuring softly to the horse as she stroked its nose.

Beautiful, strong girl . . . Such a beautiful, strong girl.

"Rose!" Bodhi saying her name shook loose her mother's voice, and Rose looked up to see that Bodhi had stopped in front of the empty stall next to Mason. "Are you okay?"

She nodded.

"Let's get her inside so I can take a look at her."

Rose stepped into the stall. When she was sure there was fresh hay on the floor, she helped Bodhi move Buttercup inside. He knelt next to the calf and felt along her abdomen while Rose stroked the animal's face.

"How bad is it?" She was asking even though she knew. What she really wanted was for Bodhi to tell her she was wrong. It wasn't so bad. It was no big deal. They'd have her back to normal in no time.

"Bad," he said, his face tight with concern. He looked up at her. "Should we get your father?"

She thought about it, imagined her dad shuffling out to the barn, looking at Buttercup with sadness, but also with apathy. She wasn't sure she could take his helplessness. Not now.

"I don't think he's going to help us here."

Bodhi nodded his understanding. She was grateful when she realized he wasn't going to challenge her decision.

"Is there a vet you can call?"

Rose bit her lip. "There is. . . ."

"What?" he asked when she hesitated.

"It's just that if I call Doc Russell, I'll have to tell my dad, and probably Marty, too."

"And that's a bad thing?"

"They won't want to save her like I do. They won't . . ." She hesitated, looking for the right word. "They won't understand."

He nodded, and for a minute, neither of them spoke.

"Is there something you can do?" Rose was surprised to hear the words come out of her mouth. Did she trust Bodhi? Did she trust him with Buttercup?

He took a deep breath and rubbed at his chin, like he was thinking about the question. She was about to repeat it when he answered.

"I can try. But you have to know there are no guarantees. Not with a vet and not with me." He met her eyes in the shadowed light of the barn.

She nodded. "I know."

He stood. "Keep her calm. I'll be right back."

She rubbed Buttercup's face while she waited, remembering when the calf had first been born, wet and angry, but fighting.

"Don't stop fighting now, girl," Rose said softly.

Bodhi returned a few minutes later, loaded down with supplies. He knelt next to the calf and quickly went to work, unraveling a feeding tube and measuring the length from Buttercup's nose to the bottom of her stomach. He added an extra foot and snipped the tube with surgical scissors.

"You have to keep her still," he said, glancing up at Rose. "She'll thrash, even sick like she is, but I need time to move the tube around, to try and find the pockets in her stomach. Okay?"

Rose nodded, wrapping her arms around the calf and bracing herself for what was next. She'd never had to help with this kind of crisis. Her dad had always been there, and when he'd needed help, he'd called one of the Breiners over, or Doc Russell if it was bad. Rose had sometimes watched from outside the stall, but she usually had to leave when things got tense. She didn't like to see the animals in pain, and although it felt cowardly, she hadn't wanted to be there in a life-or-death moment.

But now she didn't have a choice, and she tightened her arms around Buttercup, trying to fortify her resolve. "Do it," she said to Bodhi.

He forced Buttercup's mouth open and stuck the tube inside. Rose knew right when it hit the animal's esophagus, because Buttercup started thrashing, landing one quick blow to Rose's thigh before Rose tightened her grip until the calf couldn't do much more than squirm.

When all but the last foot of tubing had disappeared inside Buttercup's mouth, Bodhi paused.

"I'm going to move it around a bit, see if we can clear some of the gas in her stomach. Just keep holding her still."

Rose nodded, her arms aching, sweat dripping down her back.

He put one hand on Buttercup's belly and moved the tube slowly, gently, from side to side, waiting to see if any of the positions seemed to take down the bloat in Buttercup's belly.

"Nice and easy, girl," he said softly. "We got you."

Finally, he must have landed on a good spot, because he held it there for a minute before moving the tube again.

Rose didn't know how long they stayed that way, her body draped over Buttercup's, arms tight around the little calf's torso, hands holding its legs while Bodhi knelt in the hay next to her. It seemed like forever before Bodhi was finally retracting the tube, pulling it up bit by bit until the last of it emerged from the animal's mouth.

"Keep her still a minute so she doesn't get up and move around too fast," Bodhi said. Rose nodded, and a couple of minutes later, Bodhi spoke again. "Let her go nice and slow. Let's see if she stays calm."

Rose slowly released her grip on the animal. Buttercup stayed down, her chest rising and falling.

"Good," Bodhi said.

Rose scooted back against the wall of the barn and tried

to catch her breath. "Now what?"

"Now we wait," Bodhi said. "If she makes it through the night, I think we can say she's over the worst of it. Although we still have the feeding problem to deal with."

"I can't even think about that right now," Rose said, resting her forehead on her bent knees.

He nodded. "One step at a time."

Twenty-Eight

"It's because she was your mom's, isn't it?" Bodhi asked from the other side of the stall. "That's why you're so attached to this particular calf."

Rose didn't know how long they'd been there, but the sun had been down for hours. Bodhi left briefly to bring the other animals in, but other than that, they'd kept the vigil together.

"Yeah," Rose said. "Buttercup was the last one she really bred."

She felt rather than saw Bodhi's slow nod. Did she know him that well already?

"She's a pretty calf."

"She is," Rose agreed. "I birthed her myself."

Bodhi looked up with renewed interest. "Have any trouble?"

"A little," Rose admitted. "I had to use the calving chains."

"By yourself?" he asked.

She shrugged. "I didn't have a choice. By the time Will and Marty got here it was done."

"Did she seem sick when she was born?"

"Not really. She had a traumatic birth, but she fed right away and everything."

"Well, we have that going for us, at least," he said.

"That's what I don't understand," Rose said. "It's like she fed that one time and it was never easy again. But she shouldn't be sick. Not with bloat. It's like . . ."

"Like what?"

Rose ran her hand gently along Buttercup's back, the coarse fur tickling her palm. "It's like she just decided she doesn't want to be here or something. Like she doesn't care."

"Well, failure to thrive is a thing," Bodhi said. "Some animals just never get on their feet."

"But why this one?" Rose asked. "I did everything right."

He didn't answer right away, and she thought maybe he hadn't heard her.

"Doing everything right is no guarantee," he finally said.

Rose threw a handful of hay back onto the floor. "It's not fair."

"No. No, it's not."

The silence settled between them again. Rose thought about her dad, wading through a depression as thick as spring mud. She thought about Marty, who wasn't really happy in Milford, whatever she might say. And then there was her and Bodhi, out here with Buttercup, hoping the calf would live, and in Rose's case, trying to figure out how to live herself. It exhausted her just thinking about it, all those people fighting their battles alone in the dead of night.

"What was she like?" Bodhi's voice broke into her thoughts. For a minute, Rose wanted to pretend she didn't know who he was talking about. Then he said, "Never mind. You don't have to talk about her if you don't want to."

"I do," Rose said quickly. She sighed. "I actually really do." He waited, and she brought forward a mental image of her mother, wanting to do her justice. "She was beautiful, for starters. She had red hair—"

"Like you and Marty," Bodhi said.

Rose smiled. "Like me and Marty. She had our same green eyes, too. But she was smaller than Marty, even a little bit shorter than me. My dad was at least six inches taller. He towered over her, could scoop her up in one arm when he felt like teasing her."

"Did he do that often?" Bodhi asked.

Rose laughed a little. "All the time. Hard to imagine now, huh?"

"Not so hard," Bodhi said. "Loss changes people. Any kind of loss."

She swallowed around the lump that had risen in her throat, blinked back the tears that sprang to her eyes.

"What about you?" she asked, wanting to change the subject.

"What about me?" He'd shifted a little, and his face had moved into shadow, though she could still see his long legs stretched out in front of him.

"Have you ever lost anything?"

"You didn't finish telling me about your mom," he said. "You only told me what she looked like. If I'm going to answer your questions, you have to really answer mine."

She smiled a little. "She was . . . light."

"Light?"

"Yeah, she just had this light inside her, you know? You felt it when she was around, felt warmer and safer. And I don't think I ever saw her self-conscious. She would twirl in the fields until she fell down like a little kid, get a triple scoop of ice cream and let it drip onto her fingers, laugh so loud people turned to stare, and not always approvingly." Rose laughed at the memory.

"That's nice," Bodhi said softly. "The story about your mom, and that laugh of yours. Haven't heard it much."

"There's not much reason to laugh these days," she said, wondering why her cheeks felt warm. "Your turn." She hoped he remembered the question. It suddenly seemed too intimate to ask outright. What had she been thinking?

"I've lost stuff," he said quietly. "My mom, my dad in a different way . . ."

"I'm sorry." She meant it. She suddenly felt sorry that he'd ever lost anything, that he'd ever felt sad or alone. "You seem to be doing okay, though."

She regretted it as soon as she said it. It was something someone would say to her, and she wasn't exactly doing okay.

She sighed. "That was a dumb thing to say."

He laughed a little. "I was just getting ready to agree. I've done okay with what I was given."

"Yeah, but what is okay?" She continued without waiting for an answer. "Getting up in the morning? Going through the motions. Letting everyone else think you're okay to make things easier for them?"

"That what you're doing?"

She twisted a piece of hay around her fingers. "I don't know. Maybe."

It took him a minute to answer. "Well, for the record, it's okay to not be okay. I wouldn't be okay if I'd lost what you lost."

"You wouldn't?"

"Hell, no. And I know you have work to do, and Marty and your dad . . . I know you want them to think you're all right, but . . ." He hesitated.

"What?"

"I guess I'd like you to know that you don't have to be okay around me."

She let the words sit between them, not sure at first how to answer. What do you say when a guy—a guy like Bodhi Lowell—gives you permission to *not be okay* with him? To be yourself, even if it's messy and sad?

"Thanks," she said softly.

"Welcome." She thought she heard a smile in his voice. "How's that calf?"

"Sleeping. You should go to bed," Rose said. "I'll let you know if anything happens either way."

"I'm good," he said.

MICHELLE ZINK

"At least let me get you a drink of water or lemonade or something. I think this might go beyond your job description."

"It's exactly my job description. But I'd love some lemonade."

"I'll be right back," Rose said, standing.

He surprised her by standing and crossing to her side of the stall. She suddenly felt the raw physicality of him, like a magnetic force threatening to pull her in.

"I'll sit with Buttercup," he said, his voice a little hoarse.

She nodded, then turned to leave before he could step even closer.

She took her time going to the house, her heart beating a mile a minute, Bodhi's words echoing in her head.

I guess I'd like you to know that you don't have to be okay around me.

She poured them both some lemonade, then found the carton of chocolate-covered cherries she'd hidden on the pantry shelf. If anyone deserved to share in her secret stash, it was Bodhi. She grabbed one of her mother's old cardigans on her way out the door, breathing in the scent of lavender and vanilla as she stuffed the carton of cherries in one of the big pockets.

Loss changes people.

She opened the screen door with her hip and made her way back to the barn with the two glasses of lemonade in her hands. She passed Coco, Raven, and Mason on her way to Buttercup's stall, then stopped cold before opening the door.

Bodhi was sitting next to Buttercup, one hand on the animal's neck. His head was tipped to one side, his chest steadily rising and falling. He was asleep.

She opened the stall door as quietly as she could and stepped inside, then set one of the glasses in the hay next to him. Walking quietly around Buttercup, she lowered herself carefully next to the animal's hind legs so the calf was between her and Bodhi. She leaned back against the wall and tipped her head, taking the time to really look at him now that he was asleep.

He could have been of the earth, with his brown hair, threaded with amber, his chestnut eyes. She could smell the sweaty musk of him, breathed it in like she'd breathed in the scent of her mother. He looked so young, and for a minute, she could see the little boy he'd been in the sweep of his impossibly long eyelashes, the rise of his cheekbones, his slightly crooked nose.

She looked at his hand on Buttercup's neck, then placed one of hers on the animal's torso. She leaned back against the barn and sighed as she closed her eyes.

Twenty-Nine

Bodhi bent over the irrigation pipe, inspecting it for damage. Winter was tough on irrigation systems. They almost always required some level of repair come spring. It needed to be done, and he was glad to be out in the field where he could be alone with his thoughts.

Buttercup had made it through the night, and the animal's stomach was back to normal. Bodhi wouldn't feel like the calf was really out of the woods until she started feeding regularly and putting on weight, but the fight she'd shown so far was encouraging.

Bodhi and Rose had parted ways before the sun came up, and Bodhi had immediately headed to the fields, the irrigation system as good an excuse as any to replay the previous night and his conversation with Rose in the barn.

Now he was in a world of his own, long grass and alfalfa

swaying against his legs as he followed the irrigation lines across the field, and he thought back to the intimate moments in the barn, nothing but silence and shadows between him and Rose.

It was the nearest he'd come to feeling close to her, the closest she'd come to really opening up to him. His heart had ached when she'd talked about her mother, both because he could hear the sorrow, dark and bottomless, in her voice, and because he'd never felt that way about anybody. For the first time, he wasn't relieved by the thought. Instead it suddenly seemed like a crying shame.

That she was strong didn't surprise him. He'd seen that in her eyes from the beginning. But he hadn't fully realized the depth of her strength until she'd let him in on the extent of her sorrow. Now he had a sense of what it had cost her, getting up every day, taking care of the farm and her dad, putting a good face on things for Marty and Will.

The thought of Will made his stomach tighten. Had she put a good face on things with Will? Or were they closer than that? Had she told Will how sad she still was? He was torn between hoping she had, just so she wouldn't be alone in it, and hoping she hadn't, because he suddenly didn't want any other guy to feel as close to Rose as he had last night.

He shook his head. That was selfish. He didn't want Rose to be sad. He wanted her to find comfort with whoever she could. He was just surprised to realize he wanted it to be with him.

He caught a flash of movement out of the corner of his

eye. When he looked up from the field, he saw Rose standing near the fence. Was she watching him? A few seconds passed before she raised a hand in the air and waved. He thought she was smiling, and he raised his hand tentatively, not wanting to jump the gun in case she was waving to someone driving past on the road that ran adjacent to the Darrow property.

But when he dared a glance to his right, there was no one there, the road an empty stretch of gray in the distance.

Huh.

He looked back and she was gone. But she'd been there. That was the point. She'd been there and she'd waved.

He smiled to himself and continued down the line, working his way back toward the house. When he got near the fence where Rose had been standing, he saw something sitting on one of the posts. He walked over, wondering if she'd forgotten something.

A glass of lemonade, so cold condensation ran down its side, was sitting on top of a plate next to a sandwich and a peach. He looked around again, still wondering if Rose's generosity was meant for someone else. But then he saw the small piece of paper sticking out from underneath the sandwich.

He pulled it out and lowered his head to read the words.

Thank you.

Thirty

Rose left the plate for Bodhi on the fence post and hurried inside. It had taken twenty minutes to get up the courage to do it, and she'd been secretly relieved that he hadn't come in when he saw her. She was being stupid, but something had changed between them when they woke side by side in the barn this morning. She felt exposed, like he'd seen her naked. But that wasn't the weirdest thing; the weirdest thing was that it made her nervous and excited and scared, and somehow she didn't even mind.

Still, she was going to have to ease into this whole friendship-or-whatever-it-was-with-Bodhi thing, and she'd been happy to leave the plate and come inside, even though she paced in front of the living room window, watching as he worked his way across the field and strode toward the fence post.

He read the note, then lifted his head and glanced toward the house. She jumped back from the window, feeling like an idiot.

"Enough," she said out loud. She went to the foyer and looked up the staircase. "Dad?"

His shuffling footsteps sounded from above. A moment later, he appeared at the top of the stairs. "Everything all right, honey?"

"I just wanted to let you know I'm taking some stuff to Marty's. Do you need anything while I'm out?"

He hesitated then shook his head. Whatever he needed, Rose couldn't give it to him.

"See you in a few then," she said.

"Drive safe," he called after her as she headed to the kitchen.

She consolidated the tomatoes and blueberries she'd picked that morning into two boxes and grabbed the keys to the truck, then left through the kitchen door. Still feeling shy about leaving Bodhi lunch, she made her way to the truck through the garden, hoping to avoid him.

The coast was clear, and she set the box in the bed of the truck and got inside. A few minutes later, she was heading up the mountain, the warm summer wind blowing loose strands of hair around her face.

She thought about Bodhi and their conversation the night before. What had he meant about losing his parents? Were they both dead? He was a big guy, solid, sure. But there was something a little sad about him, too. She saw that now, and it made her regret ever being rude or unwelcoming. She'd been too wrapped up in her own loss to consider that maybe Bodhi had lost something, too.

She pulled into Marty's driveway ten minutes later, grabbed the box from the back of the truck, and headed inside.

"It's me," she said, opening the door.

"Out back!" Marty's voice drifted to her from beyond the screen door in the kitchen. "Get some iced tea and come out."

Rose set the box down on the counter and poured herself some tea from the fridge.

"Hey," she said, stepping onto the gravel pathway that led to the river at the back of the house.

Marty twisted around in the Adirondack chair to look at her. "Hey, yourself. What brings you here?"

"I brought you some blueberries and a few tomatoes," Rose said, sitting in the chair next to Marty.

"Terrific." Marty smiled. "Thank you."

"You're welcome." Rose studied the river, its current markedly slower than usual. "River's running slow."

Marty nodded. "We need rain. How's the farm?"

"Fine. Dry."

"Is it going to be a problem?" Marty asked.

"It's hard to say. We're already feeding the animals some of our reserve. It hasn't put a serious dent in our supply yet, but it will if this continues."

The Darrows supplemented the sale of their cattle by selling the hay cultivated from their grounds. But when it was dry, they had to use some of the hay to feed their own herd, which meant less revenue in the farm's coffers.

Marty sighed. "Well, keep me posted, will you?"

Rose heard the resignation in Marty's voice and felt a twinge of guilt. Farming wasn't the life for Marty, and Milford wasn't the town for her either. She was staying because of the farm, because of Rose.

"I will," Rose said, "but you should get out more if you've started worrying about the farm."

Marty laughed. "Just because I don't like farming doesn't mean I don't care about the farm."

Rose smiled. "I know that. But seriously, you're like a shut-in up here."

Marty's gaze scanned the river. "I don't think there's anything in Milford I haven't seen a thousand times, Rose."

"Yeah, but there are other places. You could go to the city, even take a trip to California or New Orleans. You always said you loved New Orleans."

It took a minute for Marty to answer. "We'll see." She leaned her head back against the chair and looked at Rose. "How's everything else on the farm?"

"Fine."

"And Bodhi? How's he working out?"

"Fine." Rose looked away. Her aunt Marty had always known her a little too well.

"Is something wrong?" Marty asked. "Is he doing his job?"

"He's fine," Rose said, then felt bad when she realized she wasn't doing him justice. "He's great actually. It's really nice to have him there, to have someone else around who knows what he's doing."

"And you two get along okay?"

Rose turned to look at her aunt. "Really?"

"What?" Marty asked innocently.

"You're not seriously trying to set me up with the farm-hand you hired for the summer, are you?"

"Well, you can't deny that he's good-looking," she said. "And he seems nice. Smart, too."

"Maybe you should go out with him," Rose suggested.

Marty laughed. "He's a little young for me. But you . . ."

Rose looked out over the water, watched it meander over rocks, making its way out to a bigger river, then the Hudson, and eventually the Atlantic. "What's the point?" she finally said.

"What do you mean?"

"He's only here for the summer. Then he'll be gone just like everyone else."

"You don't know that," Marty said. "Besides, that's not a good reason to avoid getting to know him better."

"It's good enough for me."

"Is that how you want to live, Rose?" Her aunt asked the question quietly. "Hiding from all the beauty in life because you're afraid of the hard stuff?"

"I'm just not up for another goodbye, okay?" Rose stood. "I have to go."

"Rose . . . wait . . . ," Marty protested as Rose made her way inside.

"It's okay," Rose said, still heading for the kitchen door. "I have to get back. Your stuff's on the counter."

She hurried into the house, letting the screen door slam behind her. What was the point in beauty when it was so temporary? You just got used to it, started to need it, and then it was gone.

Thirty-One

Rose's dad was standing in front of the microwave when she came in carrying two bags of groceries.

"What are you doing?" she asked him.

He looked confused, and for one terrifying minute she thought he'd really lost it.

"Heating up dinner," he said a moment later.

She set the bags on the counter. "I was going to cook."

"You were?"

"Yeah, for you and Bodhi. He's been working on irrigation all day. I figured he could use more than a warmed-up casserole. And you, too."

"Oh, I'm just fine with this, honey. Don't go to any trouble on my account," he said, opening the door of the microwave after it dinged.

"It's not any trouble." She said it softly.

He set the plate on the counter and stared down at his hands. "I know you have a lot of responsibility these days, Rosie." She blinked back the tears that rose to her eyes at the sound of the old nickname. "I'm . . ." He looked up to meet her eyes. Until lately, her dad hadn't been the kind of man to avoid anyone's gaze, but she realized now that he hadn't really looked at her in a long time. "I'm sorry. I haven't taken care of things like I should. I've been . . . your mother . . ."

She walked over and put her arms around him. "It's okay, Dad. We have Bodhi here to help out around the farm. I just miss you, that's all."

It wasn't the whole truth. Not really. She was drowning in the responsibility his depression had placed on her shoulders. But she couldn't stand to see him so sad. Sad and sorry at the same time.

"It's not okay, Rose. I know it's not okay. I'm going to get it together, I promise." He tried to smile. "I'll be riding Mason right next to you by the end of summer."

A knot of dread formed in her stomach, and she wondered if it was because she didn't believe him or because the thought of still being in Milford at the end of summer, doing the same things over and over again, made her want to scream.

"It's fine," Rose said.

He pulled away and smoothed the hair that had escaped from her braid. "Do you mind if I leave you and Bodhi to dinner? I was going to watch some TV upstairs."

She forced a smile. "Sure. I'll save you some leftovers."

He took his plate and left the room. She listened to the sound of his feet on the stairs, then turned to unpack the groceries. When she had everything laid out on the counter, she took a deep breath and reached for her mother's cookbook before she could change her mind.

She thought it would hurt. That she would be hit with something powerful, a reminder of her loss. But it wasn't like that. The memories weren't in the book after all.

She put potatoes on to boil and went to work breading chicken like her mother had taught her. While it fried, she roasted garlic to mash with the potatoes and sat at the kitchen table, snapping the ends off the long beans she'd pulled from the garden that morning. She threw a batch of cornbread in the oven while the beans steamed, then went to work cleaning up the table, changing her mind three times about which dishes to use. She didn't want to look like she was trying too hard, like this was something special she'd done just for Bodhi, but she did want it to be nice.

She thought about her conversation with Marty. She'd already decided to steer clear of Bodhi romantically. Hadn't she? Then again, just because she was making him dinner didn't mean she wanted to marry him or something. She was just being hospitable, like Marty had told her to do.

The timer buzzed on the oven and she took out the cornbread, turned off the green beans, and removed the last piece of chicken from the oil. She put everything in serving dishes and almost jumped out of her skin when she turned to take everything to the table.

Bodhi leaned in the doorway, his face already tan from the sun, his arms pulling against the fresh white T-shirt stretched across his chest.

"Oh my gosh!" Rose took a deep breath. "You scared me half to death."

The corners of his mouth turned up in a slow grin. "Sorry. I should have said something."

"Why didn't you?"

He shrugged a little. "I guess I was too busy watching you."

She let that sink in before she crossed to the table. "Irrigation repair sucks," she said, setting down the dishes. "I thought you might want something besides a casserole."

He was still smiling when she dared to look back at him. She licked her lips, floundering for something to say.

"Want some lemonade?"

His grin got bigger. "Love some."

She pulled down a glass and went to the fridge. When she turned back around, he was mercifully looking not at her, but at all the food spread out on the table.

"Wow," he said. "This looks great."

She put his lemonade on the table. "It's probably not as good as my mom's, but everything's from her recipes. And my grandmother's," she added.

He sat down and took a long drink of lemonade before digging into the serving dishes piled with food. She wondered what he was waiting for when he didn't immediately start eating, then realized he was waiting for her. She picked up her fork, and a few seconds later, he did the same.

They spent the beginning of their meal in silence. Bodhi demolished his first plate of food and immediately started dishing more. She felt another twinge of guilt watching him eat. He was obviously way overdue for a real meal, but he'd never once mentioned it.

"How's Buttercup?" she asked him as he started on his second plate.

"Better, I think. She took some milk from the bottle today."

Rose smiled. "That's great!"

He nodded. "We're not in the clear yet, but it's a good sign."

She didn't want to jinx it, but she couldn't help feeling a little relieved. One less crisis to deal with, for now at least.

"Think we'll get rain soon?" she asked.

"Anything's possible with the weather, but I don't think it's likely. National Weather Service is calling for a dry summer, and the *Almanac* backs that up."

"That's not good," Rose said.

Bodhi finished chewing. "At least you have a lot of hay stored for the herd."

"Yeah," Rose said, "but that's supposed to be for sale. It's going to hit our profit margin to use it as feed for our own animals."

He nodded slowly, and she thought she saw surprise in his eyes. "You know a lot about running the farm."

"More now than I used to," Rose confessed. "To be

MICHELLE ZINK

honest, until my mom . . . Well, I was just like every other teenage girl. On my phone and computer, listening to music, reading . . . My dad took care of the farm with help from the Breiners, and occasionally someone local to help out with hay season or vaccinations."

"And now?" he asked.

She thought about it, not wanting to seem like she felt sorry for herself. Things weren't easy, but they could always be worse. "Now I'm focusing on the farm until my dad gets back on his feet," she said. "What about you?"

He reached for the bowl of mashed potatoes and piled another heap on his plate. "What about me?"

"You seem to know a lot about farming. Do you like it?"

He seemed to think about it. "I do. It's the only place I've ever felt at home. I mean, every now and then I think it might be nice to take a break, see something new . . ."

"Why don't you?" she asked.

He hesitated. "Never found the right time."

"Is there anything else you think you'd like to do for a living?"

He grinned. "Are you asking me if I have any hobbies?"

"Maybe," she said, laughing.

"Not really. I like to read and learn. Maybe I'll go to school someday, but I think I'll always come back to farming."

She nodded. "I know what you mean. Even when you want to escape it, it's hard to imagine really leaving it behind. I guess it's in my blood."

"Mine, too," he said quietly, looking into her eyes. "You don't read anymore?"

"What?" She was still thinking about how weird it was that they could feel the exact same way about farming. Will couldn't imagine doing anything else, and Lexie couldn't imagine farming even for a day. She thought she was the only one who had mixed feelings about it.

"You said you used to read. You don't do that much anymore?"

"Not really."

"Too busy?" he asked.

"That, and too tired." She smiled. "During the school year I was getting up at four to take care of the animals, then with school and homework and everything . . ."

"But now it's summer," he said. "And I'm here."

He held her gaze, and she suddenly found it hard to breathe, like her body was so busy dealing with the butterflies in her stomach that it couldn't remember how to take in oxygen.

"Yeah," she said. "You are." She finally blinked, breathless, and got up to clear the plates. "I should have made dessert. My mom makes . . ." She froze as she set the plates in the sink.

"What?" Bodhi said softly behind her. "What does she make?"

"She *made* the best peach pie." She turned around. "Actually, I think it was her mother's recipe, but it was always my favorite, especially when she used peaches from the orchard."

"That dinner was pretty amazing," Bodhi said. "No reason you can't make a pie."

"I guess not."

He finished clearing, then stood next to her as he opened the dishwasher.

"What are you doing?" she asked him as his hip brushed hers.

"You cooked. I'm on dish duty."

She laughed. "No way. You were working all day. I went to Marty's and sat by the river, cooked a little."

He raised an eyebrow. "A little?"

"Okay, more than a little. But I got the dishes."

"We'll split it," he said. "You put the leftovers away and keep me company while I load the dishwasher."

She smiled. "Deal."

Thirty-Two

Bodhi pulled into the parking lot in front of the consignment store and reached for the cookies Rose had given him for Maggie Ryland. He caught a whiff of them from the container and Rose immediately drifted through his mind. That was her: vanilla and brown sugar, plus the sweet grass and clean water of the farm.

Not that he needed a reminder to think about Rose Darrow. In fact, she was pretty much all he'd thought about in the two weeks since they nursed Buttercup through the night. And he might be wrong, but he imagined Rose might be thinking about him, too. It was in the way she smiled at him now, minus all of the guardedness she'd shown in the beginning. Like maybe it would be okay if he really knew her. He saw it in the way she stepped into the barn in the morning, like she wanted to be there. Like maybe she even wanted to be there with him.

She'd started getting up early again, and they fed the animals and brought them out to pasture while the sun was still just a violet streak in the east. They herded like they'd been doing it together for years, then spent the rest of the day riding to the property's perimeter to repair the fences or walking the fields to repair the broken irrigation pipes. Sometimes they talked, easy now, without all the careful sidestepping that had gone into their early conversations. But just as often they didn't say a word. Sometimes Bodhi would find that a good hour had passed with them working in comfortable silence. Other times, he'd look up to find Rose staring at him. At first, she'd blushed and looked away. But lately she just smiled, like she knew he'd caught her and didn't even care.

They ate lunch together in the kitchen, working their way through the casseroles in the freezer. Rose entertained him with tales of the families who had cooked the food, and slowly, Bodhi started to feel like he knew them. After lunch they parted ways until it was time to bring the animals back in. Bodhi didn't think he'd ever looked forward to the end of the day like he did now, when he and Rose finished up outside and then ate dinner in the kitchen. Rose's dad joined them every now and then, and once, Marty, but most of the time it was just the two of them.

He smiled to himself and shook his head as he stepped out of the truck. He was halfway to the consignment store's door when a voice stopped him in his tracks.

"Bodhi Lowell."

He turned to find Will standing there, holding a bag from the pharmacy next door. "Hey, Will. What's up?"

"Not much," Will said. "You?"

Bodhi shrugged. "Paying a visit to Maggie Ryland."

"That's neighborly of you." Will's eyes dropped to the container in Bodhi's hand. "And you didn't come empty-handed, I see."

"Can't take credit for that. They're cookies from Rose."

Will nodded, then took a deep breath. "Listen, I meant what I said when we first met."

"What's that?" Bodhi asked, searching his memory.

"Rose is family," Will said. "My family. I'm not going to tell you to stay away from her. I know I don't have that right."

"That's true," Bodhi said, bracing himself for a fight.

"But I hope you'll think of her," Will continued. "She's been through a lot, and you'll be leaving at the end of summer. I don't want to see her get hurt."

"I would never hurt Rose." The words emerged a little too fiercely.

Will took his hat off, studied it in his hands. "The thing is, I know you wouldn't mean to. You don't seem like a bad guy. But I imagine you have plans after summer, and that means one way or another, you'll be leaving. It'll hurt her to get attached to you, and I know Rose; she's had about all the hurt she can take."

The anger that had been seething under Bodhi's skin left him. Will wasn't the bad guy here. He cared about Rose, and he was right. There was only one way for this to end, and that was with Bodhi leaving.

He nodded. "I appreciate the advice."

"So you'll steer clear?" Will asked.

Bodhi was a lot of things, but he wasn't a liar. "Didn't say that. But I'll think about what you said."

Will nodded and put his hat back on before turning for the parking lot.

Bodhi stood there for a minute, fighting the sinking feeling in his stomach, before continuing to Maggie's shop.

"Hey there, stranger!" Maggie greeted him when he found her at the back of the shop. The smile fell from her face. "What on earth's the matter?"

Bodhi tried to smile. "Nothing. I was in town running errands and Rose asked me to drop these off to you."

Maggie took the container of cookies out of his hand. She studied him with narrowed eyes. "Follow me."

She led him to the front of the store and pulled out a chair, then gestured for him to sit while she took two bottles of lemonade out of a little refrigerator behind the counter.

"I'm just here to drop off the cookies . . . ," Bodhi started.

"Sit."

The tone in her voice didn't leave room for any argument, and he took a seat in the wing chair while Maggie handed him one of the chilled bottles and opened the cookies. She bit into one of the cookies before leaning against the counter.

"Now what's going on? You look like you just lost your best friend."

He thought about Rose. About her smile and the way the sun made her hair shine like pennies at the bottom of a fountain. About their conversations and their silences, too.

"That's kind of inevitable," he said, staring at the bottle of lemonade in his hands. "And I think I just realized that."

"You're talking about Rose," she said softly.

He nodded. "I've been fooling myself, acting like we have all the time in the world, like this is just the beginning, when we're well on our way to the end."

"Because you're moving on after the summer?" Maggie asked.

"That's the biggest problem, yes."

"And is that set in stone?" Maggie asked. "Because I'm sure the Darrows would love to keep you on, and you could always put down roots here, get a place of your own. There are other farms in the area."

He thought about the plane ticket in his backpack. He could stay, but somehow that didn't feel right. He finally had a plan to leave, to make a break from the past that always seemed to be snapping at his heels.

"I have someplace I have to be at the end of August," he said.

"I see," Maggie said. For a minute, neither of them spoke. "So you're thinking to protect Rose from the inevitable?" she continued. "Stop your . . . friendship before she can get too attached? And you, too, I imagine."

"That's about right." He was surprised to hear her laugh. "Something funny?" he asked.

Maggie sighed and took a drink of her tea. "Can I ask you something?"

"I guess." He was agreeing, but he was already nervous.

"You think Rose is weak?"

He shook his head. "I think she's the strongest person I've ever met."

"You think she's feebleminded then?" Maggie asked.

"Feebleminded? No," Bodhi said.

Maggie gave his arm a slap. "Then why on earth would you think it's your business to make this decision—any decision—for her?"

He rubbed his arm. "I just want to protect her."

"Does she act like she needs protecting?"

He shrugged. "She acts . . . sad. I just don't want to make her sadder."

Maggie leaned in. "And what if you didn't? What if you made her happy instead? What if you made her happier than she's been since her mother died?"

"That sounds real nice, but then she'd be sad when it was over, and so would I."

"Ah, so now we're getting to the meat of it."

"What do you mean?"

"Just that maybe Rose isn't the only one you're trying to protect," Maggie said. He was getting ready to protest when she moved away from the counter. "Stay here. I want to show you something."

She returned a couple minutes later with a photograph. She handed it to him, and he saw that it was old, the colors fading, the edges turning yellow. In it a young man and woman stood with their arms around each other on the deck of a sailboat. The woman was blond and trim, her face turned up to the man, who stared down at her like he saw the moon, sun, and stars in her eyes.

"This you?" Bodhi asked.

She smiled and nodded. "Me and David."

"Was he your husband?" Bodhi asked.

"Oh no," Maggie said. "Never got that far. We only had the one summer on the Cape. Then he went to Vietnam. Didn't come back."

"I'm sorry," Bodhi said. He looked at the man, trying to see his impending death. There was nothing there. Just a man, barely out of boyhood, on a boat with the girl he loved.

Maggie looked down at the picture. "It's okay. I made peace with it a long time ago." She smiled. "I'll never forget that summer. We laughed and swam and walked on the beach until all hours of the night, talked about everything, and . . . well, you know." He heard all the things she didn't want to say in her laugh. "Then we said goodbye and he died, and I thought I might die, too. Except I didn't. I lived, and the more I lived the more I realized that David—all the beauty and loss of him—was part of that living. I married a wonderful man, had two children who drive me crazy to this day." She smiled into his eyes. "But do you think a day goes by when I wish I hadn't had that summer with David? When I would trade the pain I felt after he died for everything I felt while he was alive and we were together?"

Bodhi shook his head. "I don't imagine so, but you at least had the possibility of a future. Rose and I . . ."

"You going to drop off the face of the earth, son?" She laughed again. "Going to the moon?"

He looked down at his hands. "Not the moon, no."

"Well, the amazing thing about living in this age is there are trains and planes and something called Skype." Now it was his turn to laugh. She took his head in her hands and gave his forehead a motherly kiss. "And you know what else?"

"What?" He was barely able to choke out the word. No one had ever kissed his forehead. Not that he could remember. There was something impossibly tender about it, and he suddenly felt the loss of all the moments like it that he'd never had.

"You don't know the future," Maggie said. "I didn't know it that summer on the Cape, and you don't know it now. Anything can happen. Take hold of this moment. The future will take care of itself, with or without our help. Always does."

Thirty-Three

Rose had just gotten out of the shower when the doorbell rang. She threw on a pair of shorts and a tank top and hurried down the hall. No one ever rang the doorbell. Lexie and Will would come right in. Same with Marty, and now Bodhi.

She took the stairs two at a time, but when she opened the door, no one was there. She stepped onto the porch and almost tripped over something on the doormat. She looked down, her eyes landing on a stack of books tied together with a green ribbon.

She looked around before bending to pick them up.

A piece of stationery was tucked inside the ribbon. When she unfolded the piece of paper, she immediately recognized Bodhi's scrawl from all the times they'd worked on the farm's books, trying to reconcile their expenses with their revenue.

Always time for a good book. Especially now.
BL

She raised her head again, hoping to catch sight of him, but he'd made himself scarce in a hurry, and she turned around and went inside.

When she got back to her room, she shut the door and sat on the bed before untying the silky emerald ribbon. There were five books, all of them from the Milford library. She read the titles softly: *The Princess Bride*, *A Thousand Mornings* by Mary Oliver, *Wuthering Heights*, *Jane Eyre*, *Perfume* by Patrick Süskind.

It was an odd mix of books, and a warm flush spread through her body when she imagined Bodhi standing in the narrow stacks at the library, his shoulders spanning the space between shelves, trying to pick stuff he thought she might like. He'd done that. He'd done it for her.

She opened the books one by one, relishing the crinkle of their protective covers. She'd forgotten that about library books, the way they crinkled. She opened *A Thousand Mornings* and held it up to her nose, inhaling the scent of paper and ink.

She scooted back on her bed, taking the book with her.

I don't know where prayers go, or what they do . . .

"That was nice, you know," Rose said when they were heading to the pasture to bring in the animals later that night. "The books."

"It's nothing," he said. "I hope you like them."

He was staring straight ahead, studying the pasture like it held the answer to some kind of mystery. Was he blushing under the brim of his hat?

She smiled. "They're perfect. Every one. I already started."

He looked over at her. "Yeah?"

She nodded.

"What did you start with?"

"The poems," she said. "By Mary Oliver."

"I haven't read that one," Bodhi said. "You'll have to tell me how you like it."

"I'll pass it to you when I'm done," she said. "Then you can read it, too."

He looked over at her, and a slow smile dawned on his face. "Sounds good."

She gathered Raven's reins a little tighter in her hand. "Ready?"

He nodded, and they kicked the horses into a gallop as they headed for the cows in the distance.

Later that night, Rose was lying in bed, replaying the events of the day, trying to get comfortable in the stifling July heat. She and Bodhi had put the animals to bed and had a quiet dinner, finishing the last of the chicken pot pie she'd made the night before. She'd been enjoying cooking again. It made her miss her mom, but it made Rose feel close to her, too, flipping through the recipe book, knowing that her mom had touched the pages a thousand times, made thousands of meals from the very same book.

After dinner, they'd sat on the porch, drinking lemonade

and talking about Buttercup, who seemed to have turned a corner. She was still small, but she was eating regularly, and that was a good sign.

When they'd said good night, she'd been almost sure Bodhi was going to kiss her. He hadn't, but she had wanted him to. She had really, really wanted him to. She couldn't remember the exact moment her fear had faded into the background, the moment it had become secondary to her feelings for him, but somewhere along the way that's exactly what happened. Now she couldn't get the non-kiss out of her mind, and she finally tossed back her covers and got out of bed.

She slipped on her sneakers and crept down the hall and out the door in her boxer shorts and tank top. Stepping onto the porch, she took a deep breath. The air wasn't exactly cool, but it was fresher than the stale air in the house, and she stepped off the porch and made her way across the dirt road.

The moon was high and full, the stars like a blanket of diamonds over the clear summer sky. She'd heard kids from the city say that you couldn't see the stars there because the lights were too bright. She couldn't imagine it.

She stepped over the fence and into the orchard, weaving between the apple trees while she hummed an old song her mom used to sing when they went apple picking.

In the shade of the old apple tree,
Where the love in your eyes I could see,
Where the voice that I heard,
Like the song of a bird,
Seemed to whisper sweet music to me . . .

She was almost to the peach trees at the other end of the orchard when she heard the snap of a twig to her left. She froze.

"It's okay. It's just me."

She put a hand to her chest like that would stop the rapid beating of her heart. "Bodhi. What are you doing here?"

Thirty-Four

He had been sitting against one of the trees, eating a not-quite-ripe peach and thinking of Rose, when she'd appeared like magic. "Too hot," he said. "Couldn't sleep."

It wasn't the first time he'd come out to the orchard when he couldn't sleep. There was something kind of special about it at night, the air scented with peaches and just a hint of the apples at the other end of the orchard.

She nodded. "Me either." She made a face at the peach. "I hope you washed that."

He grinned. "Nope."

"Ew."

He laughed. "Looks like no one's tended to the orchard in a while. Figured I was safe from pesticides at least."

She nodded. "That's true."

He swept one hand out like a footman. "Care to take a seat, my lady?"

She took the tree next to him, leaning back against its trunk and peering up through the foliage over her head.

"You ever use the fruit?" Bodhi asked. "For cooking, I mean."

"Not in a while. We used to come over and pick enough for my mom to make pie, but my dad always preferred the cattle."

"Must have been a good-size operation once upon a time," Bodhi said.

She nodded. "I remember coming to Sunday dinner when my grandparents still owned it. There were lots of farmhands who worked here in the summer, both with the animals and in the orchard."

"Could be that way again someday," Bodhi said.

She didn't say anything for a minute, and he wondered if he'd touched a nerve. "Maybe."

"You could make the peach pie at least," he suggested.

She looked over at him and laughed. "I think you might have your own reason for suggesting the pie."

He grinned. "I might."

They sat in silence for a few minutes, but it wasn't one of the awkward silences from their beginning. Instead it felt totally natural to be sitting next to her in the dead of night, talking about the farm and peach pie and the way things had once been and might be again.

"What about you?" she asked, turning to him. "What was your childhood like?"

His throat constricted, everything in his body rebelling against telling her the truth. He passed another peach from hand to hand, feeling the barely there fuzz of it against his palms. If he told her, would she ever look at him again the way she'd finally started to look at him these past couple of weeks? Would she see the Bodhi who knew his way around a farm, who liked to read and learn? Or would she instead see Bodhi the High School Dropout? Bodhi the Loser?

"I'm sorry," she said softly. "You don't have to talk about it if you don't want to."

Then again, this was him. He'd never before apologized for who he was. No sense starting now. She'd find out eventually anyway.

"It's okay," he said quietly. "It's just not a pretty story, that's all."

"I don't need pretty stories." He turned to look at her, and she was staring right at him through the darkness, her head still against the trunk of the peach tree, hair tumbling down her shoulders.

"My dad's a drunk," Bodhi said. "Has been for as long as I can remember. There were lots of 'accidents' growing up— running into doors, falling down stairs, that kind of thing."

"He hurt you?" she asked softly.

"I got used to the physical stuff." He cleared his throat. "But he wasn't exactly equipped to take care of me, you know?" He continued without waiting for her to say anything. "I left when I was fourteen. Never looked back."

He heard her surprise in the intake of her breath. "Fourteen . . . that's so young. What did you do?"

"Wasn't easy at first," he admitted. "I wasn't really

equipped to take care of myself either. But small town people tend to be generous, and that's where I headed when I was trying to lay low, keep from getting sent to foster care or back to my dad. I got some work, little stuff at first in exchange for room and board, and eventually I guess you could say I actually knew what I was doing."

"But didn't anyone want to call the police? Or Child Protective Services?"

"In the beginning, I think my bruises told the only story they needed to hear. Later, after I grew some, it was easy to lie about my age. Don't need working papers on most farms."

"Then what?" she asked.

He took a deep breath. "I worked. I learned. I got my GED. Kept working. Kept learning." He turned to smile at her. "Now I'm here."

She returned his smile before her expression grew serious again. "What about your mom?"

"She left when I was little," Bodhi said. "I don't really remember her, but I can't imagine she was anything special."

"Why do you say that?" she asked.

"She left, didn't she?"

"That doesn't mean she didn't love you. Maybe she wanted something better for you. Maybe she was setting herself up to give you a better chance."

"Then why didn't she come back?" He turned his head to look at her, wondering what he would see in her eyes. But she was still Rose, and she still looked at him just the same.

"I don't know," she said softly.

The silence stretched between them. Bodhi let it sit, listened to an owl in the distance, the faint scuffle of a squirrel or mouse nearby.

"Do you ever get scared?" she suddenly asked. "I mean, you know, scared that you'll just keep doing the same thing or that nothing will change? Or maybe that everything will change?"

Tell her, a voice said in his head. *Tell her you're leaving. That you do get scared; scared you'll never see her again, scared you won't even get to love her in the here and now because once she knows you're leaving, she won't want anything to do with you. Tell her you've never been so scared of anything in all your life.*

"I do," she continued. "And I think I'm just now beginning to admit it to myself."

"What are you afraid of?" He didn't know why the other words wouldn't come out.

"The truth?" she asked.

He met her eyes. "Always."

"All of it. Things changing, things staying the same. Most of all, I think I'm just afraid of people leaving, you know?" She said the last part quietly, like maybe she hadn't realized it until this moment. "People say they won't, but no one can promise that, can they? People get sick and die or they get in accidents or something else happens and they just have to go. No one can really say they'll never leave you and mean it."

He thought he might choke on the words in his throat. He spoke around them instead. "It's part of life, I guess." He felt like a jerk. Telling her something that would make caring about him okay without telling her the rest of it.

But he couldn't. Not right now. He needed to think it through more. Find the best way to tell her. She'd had enough hurt. Enough of people leaving.

"I guess," she said. "But it sucks."

"I can't say that I disagree."

They sat there for a few minutes longer before she got up, brushing the dirt off the back of her legs. "I better get back. We have to be up in a few hours."

"You should sleep in," he said. "Let me handle the animals in the morning."

"No way." She looked down at him. "You coming?"

"I think I'll stay for a bit," he said.

"Maybe you should sleep in tomorrow," she said. "Let me handle the animals in the morning."

He smiled. "No way."

She started walking, holding up a hand as she went. "See you soon."

Thirty-Five

"Would you like more cake, John?" Maggie asked Rose's father.

"I wouldn't mind some, if there's enough, that is."

Rose tried to keep her face impassive. It was just cake, and it's true that she had kind of guilted her dad into coming to dinner at Maggie's house, that he still looked pale and thin, but at least he was participating.

Maggie had called earlier in the week to invite them—Bodhi included—to dinner. Rose had tried hedging, but Maggie Ryland wasn't someone who took no for an answer, and before Rose knew it, she was agreeing to be there promptly at seven p.m. on Friday.

Her dad had been quiet through dinner, but he'd answered Maggie's questions and tried to smile at all the right times. It was something.

"I just don't know what is going on with this weather," Maggie was saying. "Haven't had a lick of rain in three months."

"It's hurting us on the farm," Rose said. "We're feeding the herd our own hay."

"Well, that can't be good for business," Maggie said, pouring more coffee. "What will you do?"

"Pray for rain," Bodhi said. "Not much else we can do."

Maggie took a sip of her coffee. "Well, I hope it happens soon. My flowers are barely surviving, and I'm worried about watering them too much. Don't want the well to run dry. Although I realize that's a small concern when compared to the farm."

Rose smiled. "Not small at all. The garden is beautiful. You must have put a lot of work into it."

Maggie laughed. "If that's work, I'd happily work all day. It's the only thing that keeps me sane now that Frank is gone. That and the store and this old place. They keep me busy enough."

"Mr. Ryland was a nice man," Rose said. She remembered him as a barrel-chested firefighter with a voice—and a laugh—that carried. "He always brought candy to Fire Prevention Day at school."

Maggie smiled. "That man could eat sugar like a six-year-old. He probably told you he bought it for you. More than likely it was from the stash he kept in his truck. The one he thought I didn't know about."

They laughed, and even Rose's dad smiled a little.

"The garden sure is nice this time of night," Maggie said. "Why don't we sit outside for a bit?"

Rose had planned an early getaway. Dinner and conversation with Maggie and then right back to the farm. It had been a while since she'd felt normal around other people, and she hadn't expected to feel that way tonight. She still missed her mom, still hurt when she thought about her. But it was nice to be somewhere other than the farm, to be talking to Maggie and laughing over dessert with her father and Bodhi like nothing tragic had happened to them. She hadn't forgotten, but she had set it aside a little to make room for something else, and so far nothing terrible had happened.

"That would be nice," Rose said. She looked from Bodhi to her dad. "That okay with you guys?"

Her dad nodded. "I think that will be just fine."

"I've got nowhere to be but here," Bodhi said.

It was something she liked about him: how he always seemed present. She never felt like there was anything more important than the moment they shared, even if it was an unremarkable one.

They moved outside to the porch. Her father started to sit on one of the wicker chairs, but Maggie stopped him by speaking gently. "John, I was wondering if I could ask you to take a look at our mower. Darn thing was giving me trouble the other day."

A look of panic crossed her father's features before he could compose himself. "Oh, I think Bodhi might be a better man for the job."

Maggie smiled. "Now, no offense to Bodhi"—she cut a glance at him—"but I think you might have a few years' experience on him, John." She touched his arm lightly. "Would you?"

Rose watched her dad's face, wondering if he might just say no, he wasn't up to it, he just couldn't. But a moment later resignation passed over his features and he nodded. "I'd be happy to."

"Wonderful." Maggie turned to Bodhi and Rose. "You two enjoy the swing. There are drinks in the house if you get thirsty."

Rose watched them walk toward the outbuilding that acted as Maggie's garage. They disappeared into the shadows a minute later.

"Wow," Rose said. "This might be the first thing he's done besides eat, read, and watch TV since . . . since my mother died."

"That bad, huh?" Bodhi's voice was soft next to her.

She nodded, turning to look at him. "Yeah."

"I'm sorry," he said. "It must be hard for you."

The words didn't prompt her usual defensiveness. Maybe it's because of the way he'd said it, like it was just a fact. Not a reason to pity her or something to be sad about, just the way things were.

"It has been." She almost held her breath, expecting some momentous occurrence in the wake of the confession. But the ground didn't crack beneath her. There was no thunder, no hurricane. Just a kind of calm. "I thought it was temporary at first. You know, that he was just sad right after the funeral."

"But he didn't get better," Bodhi said.

She looked down at her sandaled feet, swinging gently over the floorboards of the porch next to Bodhi's big boots. "If anything, he got worse. Right after she . . . well, right after she died, he was busy. There were people at the house and arrangements to make, then the funeral, and for a while after that, people still came over at all hours."

"Trying to keep you both busy."

Rose nodded. "But eventually everyone had to get back to real life, and honestly, I was ready for them to be gone. Living like that, with everyone at the house all the time, bringing food and asking what they could do for us . . . I don't know. It's like her death didn't really seem real until they went away. For a while, I was glad to put it off, but at some point, I guess I just needed to feel it." She turned to look at him. "You know?"

"Can't move on until you let yourself feel it," he said softly.

"Exactly. That's exactly it." She laughed a little. "Not that I've really moved on. But things are better than they were during the winter."

He looked out over Maggie's darkened garden. "She passed in January?"

"January fifteenth." Rose remembered the morning like it had happened yesterday. The sky dark and heavy, snow falling softly outside her mother's bedroom window as a candle flickered on her bedside table. "After the funeral, after everyone went home . . ." She sighed. "It's hard to explain." She was surprised to feel him take her hand.

"Try," he said, his voice gruff.

"Well, it felt like I was the only person in the whole world. I'd get up to take care of the animals, and it was just . . . dark. Sometimes it would be snowing when I headed for the barn, and it was just me and the animals and not another sound in the world. At first I thought it was the farm. Just . . . being alone there with my dad so depressed, but it was like a bubble that I carried with me, so that even when I was at school or with Will and Lexie, I felt apart from them, like I couldn't quite reach them." She looked at him. "After a while, I got used to it, stopped trying to break through it."

"I wish I'd been here," he said, his eyes locked on hers.

It took her a few seconds to answer. "Me too."

She felt herself pulled toward him with a force so powerful, denying it wasn't even a possibility. She could see the flecks of amber in his eyes, feel the soft exhale of his breath. His face was inches from hers when Maggie's voice came from the shadows.

"There, now!" Rose and Bodhi pulled away from each other.

Rose swallowed, smoothing the skirt of her sundress. "You fixed it, Dad?"

Her dad stepped into the light of the porch. "Yep. Just a loose wire."

Maggie laughed. "Don't I feel like a dunce." She smiled. "Sorry to leave you two alone."

Bodhi shifted awkwardly next to her.

"It's no problem," Rose said.

"I'm glad," Maggie said. "Let me wrap you up some cake to take home."

She met Rose's eyes on her way into the house, and for a split second, Rose was certain Maggie winked at her.

Thirty-Six

Rose was watering the garden the next afternoon when Bodhi came around the corner, his hat in his hand.

"Hey," he said, taking a swipe at his brow.

She smiled, feeling a little shy after their moment on the swing. "Hey. How's the irrigation system looking?"

He came closer, and she caught a whiff of laundry detergent, sweat, and something deep and musky that she was coming to associate with Bodhi. It made her a little light-headed.

"Not bad," he said. "Should be done next week. Which will be about right to start cutting."

Rose nodded. The only upside to the lack of rain was that the fields were dry, the only time you could really cut hay. On the other hand, they were blowing through their stash feeding the herd, who could no longer get what they needed from the dried-out grass in the pastures.

"Mind if I take a drink?" Bodhi asked, tipping his head at the hose in her hand.

"Sure. I have to check on the tomatoes anyway."

She handed him the hose and walked about halfway down the row of tomato plants. She was kneeling in the dirt, trying to figure out why one of the drip hoses wasn't working, when she felt a sprinkle on her back.

She looked up, a flutter of hope rising inside her. Maybe it was going to rain.

But no. There wasn't a cloud in the sky.

She bent her head back to the hose. A few seconds later a short blast of water hit her from behind.

"What the . . . ?!" She stood up, holding out her dripping arms as she glanced at Bodhi, standing there with a mischievous grin on his face. "Was that *you*?"

He shrugged, then turned the hose on her full blast, hurrying down the pathway for even better access.

She shrieked, taking cover behind the tomato plants, which got an even bigger dose of water as Bodhi sprayed her from the other side of the row.

"Oh my god!" She was soaked, water dripping from her braid down into her shirt, which was plastered to her body. "What are you *doing*?"

He shrugged. "Just helping you cool off, that's all."

She shook her head, trying to keep a smile from rising to her lips. "You are *so* going to pay for that."

She ran to the end of the row and came around, rushing

Bodhi for the hose even as he continued spraying her, Rose shrieking and both of them laughing. When she finally got close enough to make a grab for the hose, he held it above his head, seemingly oblivious to the fact that he was getting soaked, too.

She reached up, stretching out to try and get ahold of the hose, and for a split second, their bodies were pressed together, the water spraying around them, and Rose didn't even care. Not one bit.

"Rose?" They both turned toward the voice. "What's going on?"

Will stood by the gate, a look of confusion on his face.

"Will . . . We were just . . . I was watering the garden and—"

His eyes ran over their wet bodies. "Watering the garden, huh?"

"Hold on," she said, trying to compose herself. "Let me get a towel and I'll be right back."

"You know what, Rose?" he said, his face turning still and hard in a way she'd never seen. "Forget it."

He turned, heading toward the orchard and pond that separated their properties.

"Will!" she called after him. "Will, wait!"

But he just kept walking.

Rose pulled her wet shirt away from her body a little, wringing out some of the water while she fought the feeling that someone had her heart in a vise.

Bodhi walked back to the faucet and turned off the hose.

"You okay?" he asked her.

She wiped the water from her face. "I just . . . I have to go talk to him."

Bodhi nodded. "Can I help?"

She shook her head and started for the kitchen door. "I'm going to change. I'll see you later."

He was still standing there holding the hose when she stepped into the house. She hurried upstairs and into her room, Will's expression frozen in her mind. Why had he looked hurt? And even confused?

She peeled off her wet clothes and dried her body before throwing on her shorts and a tank top.

Will didn't have a right to be hurt. They were just friends. Right?

She thought back to Lexie's words in the truck on the last day of school. Was there any possibility Lexie had been right? That Will was in love with her?

She stood there in the middle of her room, her concern for Will morphing into something like anger. He didn't have a right to be upset. She had never given him a sign that they were anything more than friends. Who did he think he was? Busting in on her and then acting all mad, like he was her boyfriend or something?

She grabbed her phone and took the stairs two at a time, letting the screen door bang behind her. She went to the barn and saddled up Raven, then hopped on the horse's back and headed across the dirt road.

She waved to Will's dad as she made her way across

their east pasture. He pointed to the milking barn, and Rose nudged Raven into a gallop as they headed that way.

She found Will halfway down the galley, kneeling in the hay on the floor and looking at an electronic milker with one of the guys who worked on the Breiners' farm. Will glanced up as she approached, then turned his attention back to the contraption in his hands like he hadn't seen her.

"Will . . ." She stopped right next to him. She was almost shaking with anger, both because of the way he'd acted when he'd seen her and Bodhi and because he was ignoring her now. "We need to talk."

"I'm busy," he said.

"That's bull, Will, and you know it." She put her hands on her hips. "Now stop acting like a baby and talk to me."

He stood, handing the milker to the man at his side, who looked away, obviously embarrassed to be witnessing the confrontation.

"Check the supply shed for that part," Will told him. "I'll be along in a bit."

The guy nodded, and with one more glance at Rose, walked away.

Will brushed the hay and dirt off his hands. "What do you want?"

"What do I want?" she asked. "Really?"

He shrugged. "What else do you want me to say?"

"Why are you acting this way? I don't . . . I don't know what you want from me."

He looked at her, anger flashing in his blue eyes. "What I

want from you? Like it's some kind of chore?"

"That's not what I mean and you know it!"

"Then what do you mean, Rose?"

She took a deep breath, trying to think through what she was about to say. "I just don't . . . You're obviously mad about . . . about Bodhi. But you and me, we're friends."

His jaw seemed to harden. "We're more than friends."

She nodded. "You're right. We're family, like you said. You're like a brother to me."

"A brother?" He laughed, but it was as hard as the sun-cracked ground outside. "A brother. That's great. That's just great, Rose."

"What? I don't know why you're mad!"

"You really think that's what I meant when I said we were family? That you were like a *sister* to me?"

"I don't know . . . I guess."

"Well, that's not how I feel, Rose. And I thought you felt something more for me, too."

She looked down at her legs, bare above her boots. "But you never said anything."

"I didn't think I had to," he said. "I was just trying to give you some space, that's all."

She swallowed hard. "I'm sorry. I didn't know."

He hesitated. "And now that you do?"

She kicked her feet around in the straw. "I don't . . . I don't know."

"It's him, isn't it?" Will almost spat the words. "Bodhi Lowell?"

"I don't know," she said softly.

"Well, what do you know, Rose?"

She flinched as he shouted the words, and the rise in his voice brought back all her old anger. "I know that you don't have a right to be mad! Or to tell me who I can care about or who I can spend time with! I know that you can't expect me to be a mind reader, and you can't come in like some caveman now that there's somebody else in the picture!"

He crossed his arms over his chest. "So that's it, then? Bodhi is officially in the picture?"

"I don't know," she said. "But I do know that I deserve to be happy. And I don't answer to you."

She turned away, stalking to the front of the barn where Raven waited.

"He's going to hurt you, Rose," Will called after her. "He's going to leave and he's going to hurt you."

Sadness mingled with her anger as she climbed into Raven's saddle, but she didn't know if it was because she'd hurt Will or because deep down she knew he was right.

Thirty-Seven

"I think a pink, feathered, sequined lamp is a requisite for my room, don't you?" Lexie held up the monstrosity for consideration.

"Um, only if you want to look like a fifth grader on crack," Rose said.

Lexie scowled. "More is more, haven't you heard?"

Rose ran a hand over the smooth metal of a lamp whose base was shaped like the Eiffel Tower. "Must have missed the memo."

They were at Bed Bath & Beyond, shopping for things Lexie's mother probably wouldn't let her buy for her apartment in the city. If it were up to Lexie's mom, it would be all plastic bins and comforters with polyester fill, something that made Lexie shudder. She'd been slowly adding to the college stash with her babysitting money.

"All right," Lexie said, "I'll wait on the lamp. Let's go look at bathroom stuff. I need a shower caddy, preferably something no one else will have."

Rose laughed as she pushed the cart. "We're at Bed Bath & Beyond, not Versace. I think your odds of finding something original are slim to none."

"A girl can dream," Lexie said. "Besides, why are we talking about shower caddies when you never finished telling me about the Will thing?"

"I did finish," Rose said. "We had a fight and I left. That's all there is to tell."

Lexie veered down the candle aisle.

"Can you even have candles in your room?" Rose asked.

"I'm just looking," Lexie said. "So you didn't make up or anything after?"

"Nope," Rose said. "And I'm not apologizing. He's in the wrong."

"He totally is in the wrong," Lexie said. "But it's Will. Do you really want to fight with him like this?"

Rose thought about it. "I honestly don't care right now. Maybe we just need some space from each other."

"Well, I hate to say I told you so," Lexie said, adding a pomegranate-scented candle to the cart. "But I've known Will was in love with you since the day we met."

"Gloating is so unattractive," Rose said, steering them toward the bathroom section.

"So does this mean you and Bodhi are, like, a thing?" Lexie asked.

MICHELLE ZINK

"I don't know," Rose said. "I mean, there's definitely something there. I think."

Lexie raised an eyebrow. "You think?"

"Well, he hasn't said it or anything, so I can't be sure. But he did hold my hand at Maggie's the other night out on the porch."

"Really?"

Rose nodded.

"He's into you then." Lexie picked up a set of six-hundred-thread-count sheets. "I wonder why these don't come in twin size," she muttered.

"Probably because you should be able to afford a decent-size bed before you spend two hundred dollars on sheets."

Lexie narrowed her eyes. "I think you've gotten funnier."

"If you say so."

Lexie put the sheets back and moved to a more reasonable three-hundred-thread-count set. Rose groaned. "We've been here for nearly two hours. How much more stuff do you need to look at?"

"Don't complain," Lexie said. "At least it's air-conditioned in here."

"True."

"So what are you going to do about it?" Lexie asked.

"About the air-conditioning?"

Lexie rolled her eyes. "About Bodhi."

"Nothing. I mean, what can I do? I'm going to wait and see what happens."

"Well, don't wait too long," Lexie said. "We're halfway

through summer already."

The thought caused a shadow of dread to pass over Rose's mood. She was right. Bodhi would be leaving soon. Even if he felt the same way, their time together was rapidly dwindling.

Two hours later, Lexie dropped her off at home. Rose watched her leave, the car kicking up a cloud of dust in its wake.

Being back outside after spending the afternoon in air-conditioned bliss was like stepping from a meat locker into an oven. Rose looked up at the sky where billowy clouds sat over the mountain. The forecast called for a thirty percent chance of rain, but she didn't want to get her hopes up. She went inside and threw on her bathing suit, then headed for the pond.

Thirty-Eight

Bodhi spent the day finishing the irrigation repair, then went over the books. He was worried about the farm's finances. Marty left him a paycheck in the kitchen every Friday, but the profit-and-loss statement was more loss than profit. Normally, he wouldn't be concerned. He'd start cutting hay soon, and then the Darrows could sell some of it to bring themselves more solidly into the black. But the herd was going through the stored hay at an alarming rate, and if they didn't get rain soon, the Darrows would have to set aside some of the new hay for feed as well.

It was late afternoon by the time he headed back up to his room. The hayloft felt thirty degrees hotter than the temperature outside, but he sat down at his computer anyway, trying to distract himself. As soon as his inbox opened, he saw the name: CBurton4298@gmail.com.

His heart raced as he opened the message.

Hi there, Bodhi,
Still no sign of your dad. I'd be worried if he hadn't said he
was trying to find you. Any sign of him yet?
Christine

Bodhi thought back to all the people he'd worked with in
the months before he'd left for New York. Had he told any
of them he was going to work for the Darrows? Had he left
a trail his dad might be able to follow? He chewed his lip,
thinking.

He didn't think so. He'd grown used to being cautious, a
product of leaving home at such a young age and having to
stay under the radar. Still, the thought of his dad out there
looking for him made him vaguely sick to his stomach.

He realized sweat was rolling down his temples, his
shirt sticking to his upper body like a second skin. It was too
damn hot. He couldn't think.

Closing the laptop, he climbed down from the loft and
headed to the barn. He saddled Mason, feeding the horse
a carrot he'd taken from the kitchen at lunch, and headed
across the orchard to the pond, his mind churning with all
the scenarios that might result if his dad found him after all
these years. Maybe his dad just wanted to reconnect. Maybe
he *had* changed.

Bodhi allowed Mason to pick his way up the hill on
his own steam. When they got to the top, Bodhi saw that
he wasn't the only one desperate to cool off; Rose was float-
ing on her back in the middle of the pond, her eyes closed
against the sun, slightly shadowed behind a few clouds that

had drifted in front of it.

"You always in the habit of watching people sleep?"

Her voice startled him from his reverie. He'd been staring.

"Uh . . . I was . . . I didn't know . . ."

She righted herself, grinning at him while she treaded water. "I'm just giving you a hard time."

He sighed his relief, and gave Mason some lead to make his way down the hill

"Hot, right?" she said.

"Hot doesn't quite cut it," he said, stopping the horse at the edge of the pond.

"Well, are you going to stand there, or are you coming in?" she asked him.

"I . . . uh . . ." He cleared his throat. "I didn't bring a suit."

Her smile got bigger, although he didn't think it was the sun that turned her cheeks pink. "You were going to *skinny-dip*? In broad daylight?"

"No! I have . . . um . . . boxers." Why was he so flustered? It's not like he hadn't swum in boxers before. Not like he hadn't skinny-dipped with a girl for that matter. But this was Rose, and somehow he didn't want to do any of the things with her the way he'd done them with other girls.

"Aren't boxers kind of like a bathing suit?"

He thought about the thin fabric of his boxers.

"I'll turn my back while you get in," she suggested. "Will that work?" When he didn't answer, she sighed. "It's hot, Bodhi. Come on. It'll be fine."

She turned her back, treading water while she faced the tree line of the woods that backed up to the pond.

He only hesitated a minute. She was right; it was hot. And once he was in the water, what would it matter?

He dismounted, tying Mason to one of the trees, then pulled off his jeans and T-shirt. He hadn't felt self-conscious around a girl since he was a kid, but he was self-conscious now, and it didn't seem to matter that Rose's back was turned.

He thought about stepping in slow, then decided to put himself out of his misery instead. He dove in from one of the rocks that jutted out over the water. When he came up, Rose was squealing.

"Couldn't you have dived in a little farther away?" she asked, laughing. "You seem determined to get me wet!"

He laughed. "You're in the water already."

He dove under, opening his eyes and making for her bare legs. He gave one of her feet a gentle tug as he swam by, and when he came up, she put her hands on his shoulders and tried to dunk him.

They swam around each other, dunking and splashing, laughing and shouting. They raced from one end of the pond to the other, tying it up in the first two races and finishing it in a tie breaker won by Rose. But just barely.

They both dove under, swimming back to the other side of the pond, emerging only a foot apart in chest-deep water. And then she was right there, so close he could see the water beading on her upper lip, the filtered sun casting faint shadows on her bare shoulders.

It wasn't that far from one side of the pond to the other, but they were both breathing hard, their eyes locked.

She reached for him, wrapping her arms around his shoulders, pressing her chest to his. Her face was so close he could feel her breath against his mouth.

"Rose . . ." He didn't want to hurt her. Didn't want to leave her. But he would do both, and he hadn't even warned her.

She put a finger to his lips. "Shhhh . . ."

And then he didn't know who did it, who moved closer, who eliminated the space between them, but his mouth was on hers, her legs wrapped around his waist, and it was like she'd always been there. Like she'd always been a part of him.

He kissed her like his life depended on it. Maybe it did.

He didn't know how long they stood there, intertwined like the trunks of two willow trees he'd once seen in Texas, but they didn't move until the sky opened up above them, rain splattering the water intermittently at first, and then, all at once, in a downpour.

Thirty-Nine

Rose pulled into an open spot in front of Sweet Clementine's and hopped out of the truck. She was early, but she went in anyway and spent the next ten minutes talking to Marie about the farm, the weather, and the one bit of rain they had gotten two weeks earlier.

"You look happy," Marie had said when she mentioned the rain.

Rose hadn't been aware that she was smiling, but she could never think about that day without remembering the first time she and Bodhi had kissed. They'd done a lot of kissing since, though he'd been respectful enough not to push for anything else. Sometimes too respectful, she thought.

Still, the last two weeks had been the best of her life. They laughed and talked, stealing kisses behind the barn, in the orchard, even on top of their horses while they dealt with the herd. He left something on the porch for her almost every day—a new book, a wild buttercup, a bunch of hay twisted into a heart that now adorned the wall above her bed. One time he even left her a bushel of peaches he'd picked at the orchard, and for the first time since her mother had died, she made peach pie. It hadn't been exactly the same, but for a minute, it was like her mother was right there with her. Bodhi had given her that and so much more.

She couldn't think about him—about his smile and the way he looked at her, about the special light in his eyes or the way his arms felt around her, the way his heart seemed to beat in time with her own—without smiling. She felt like she'd come out of hibernation. She still missed her mom, but after months in the shadows, she finally felt like she was walking in the sun again.

"Hey, you!" The bell on the door jingled as Marty stepped inside the café. "Am I late?"

Rose shook her head. "I was early."

"And I've been talking her ear off," Marie said.

Rose laughed. "Not at all. It was nice to have the company."

Marie waved at the nearly empty restaurant. "Take a seat wherever you like. I'll bring you some water and menus."

They chose a seat near the window. After they ordered, Marty took a long sip of her iced tea, studying Rose over the rim.

"What?" Rose asked.

"You look different," Marty said.

Rose self-consciously touched her braid. "Do I?"

Marty nodded. "I can't put my finger on it."

Rose shrugged. "I don't know. I'm wearing my hair the same way I always do, and I've had these clothes forever."

Marty adjusted her silverware. "I asked you here to apologize."

It took Rose a second to realize Marty was actually talking to her. "Apologize? Why?"

"I made you unhappy the last time we talked." She met Rose's gaze. "I pushed, and I'm sorry."

They'd seen each other in passing when Marty came to leave Bodhi's check every Friday, but they hadn't really talked since the day at Marty's house when they'd argued.

"It's okay," Rose said.

Marty shook her head. "No, it's not."

"Marty, it's okay." Rose smiled.

"Wait . . ." Marty sat back in her chair, a slow dawning on her face. "Do you mean . . . ?"

Rose nodded. "You were right."

"I was right!"

Marie appeared at the table and set down their salads. "Imagine that, Marty. We old women are actually right sometimes."

Marie had no idea what they were talking about, but Rose still laughed.

"So does this mean what I think it means?" Marty asked.

Rose picked up her salad fork. "I'm not sure. I mean, we're . . . you know . . . together, but . . ."

"How together is together?"

"Marty!" Rose felt her cheeks get warm. "That's none of your business."

"Fine," Marty said, digging into her salad. "But it's good? You're happy?"

Rose took a deep breath. "I am."

"But?"

"I just don't know what's next. I mean, he's leaving at the end of August."

"Maybe you should stay in the moment," Marty said. "You've had a rough few months. Take your joy where you can find it."

Rose finished chewing. "I know. It's just hard not to think about the future, you know?"

"I do know," Marty said. "But trust me; it won't change anything. You can't anticipate all the things that might happen between now and then. Worrying about them is a waste of the joy you have now."

Rose grinned. "Someone's been meditating."

"Don't knock it, kiddo."

"I would never," Rose said. She hesitated before speaking again. "Have you been in love, Aunt Marty? Since Larry, I mean."

The ghost of a smile touched Marty's lips. "There was someone. In Chiang Mai."

"What was his name?"

"Tseng."

"What happened?" Rose asked.

Marty seemed to think about it. "He got a job offer in London. I decided to come home." She shrugged a little. "Not everything is meant to last forever."

The words dropped like a stone in Rose's stomach. Did she want her and Bodhi to last forever? Is that why she was scared? Because she knew instinctively that things like that just didn't happen at her age?

"You didn't want to go with him?" Rose asked. "To London, I mean."

"I didn't know what I wanted."

"And now?" Rose was almost afraid to hear the answer. She didn't want Marty to leave again, but she also didn't like the sadness that had crept into her aunt's eyes when she talked about Tseng.

Marty smiled a little. "Still not sure."

Marie brought their sandwiches and refilled their iced tea, then left them alone again. Rose was still thinking about Marty and Tseng, imagining Marty in love in a foreign land, riding on the back of some guy's motorcycle, her hair streaming out behind her like a banner.

"How's the little calf?" Marty asked, taking a bite of her sandwich.

"She's actually better," Rose said. "She had a rough spell, but we got her through it. She's even eating more regularly now."

"I'm glad to hear it. I know you have a soft spot for that one."

Rose looked down at her plate, thinking of her mother

standing next to the animals, petting them with a light in her eyes that made it clear there was nowhere else she'd rather be.

"I do," she said.

"Your mom was good at breeding," Marty said. "Always was, even when we were kids. She used to go to the auctions with Pop, and I'd swear she just knew which animals were the best. At first, Dad just indulged her, picking up a cheap little heifer here and there to humor her. But she was always right, and after a while Dad started to really listen."

Rose nodded. "The animals liked her, too. I think Coco's sad."

"Have you been riding her?" Marty asked.

Rose shook her head.

"She needs the exercise, Rose. Have Bodhi do it if you can't. Your mom loved that horse. She shouldn't be cooped up in the barn now that the weather is better. The sun will do her good." She grinned. "It sure has done you some good."

"Very funny." But Rose couldn't help smiling. Marty was right; she needed to take her joy where she could find it.

Forty

"I can't believe you're moving now," Rose said, collapsing on the couch in Lexie's new living room in the city. "I thought we had the rest of the summer."

"I know," Lexie said. "But it's almost August, and my mom thinks I need some time to get settled, get to know my roommates, et cetera."

Rose grabbed one of the throw pillows and hugged it to her chest. "Well, it sucks."

She'd driven down early that morning with Lexie and her parents to help Lexie move in. They'd met Lexie's new roommate, a tiny blonde named Madison, and spent the rest of the day arranging Lexie's room and unpacking her clothes. Now it suddenly seemed too real. Lexie's parents would come back with takeout, they would eat lunch around the tiny table in the living room, and then Rose would ride home with Lexie's parents while she started her new life in the city.

Rose was still a little envious, but having Bodhi waiting for her on the farm softened the blow. She still didn't know what the future held for them, but she'd spent the last few days trying to follow Marty's advice by staying in the moment. Besides, she reasoned, maybe Bodhi would decide to stay. It's not like he had a family waiting for him somewhere. Maybe he'd *want* to stay.

Lexie rested her head on the back of the couch and turned to look at Rose.

"You'll come stay with me?"

"Of course," Rose said.

"Promise."

Rose smiled. "I promise."

"And you'll think about getting out of that town? I mean, I know you have a hunk of burning love now—"

Rose laughed. "I *know* that isn't a saying from Grandma Russell."

Lexie looked offended. "I heard it in an old song when my dad had control of the radio in the car. Anyway, my point is, I know you have a hot guy and everything, but don't forget about you. About what you want. Okay?"

"What if they go together?" Rose asked her. "The hot guy and the things I want."

Lexie grinned. "Even better. Just don't lose you, Rose. Because I like you."

She leaned her head on Lexie's shoulder. "I like you, too."

"Have you talked to Will yet?" Lexie asked a few seconds later.

"No."

"Are you going to?"

"I don't know," Rose said. "I don't know how to talk to him now that the thing with Bodhi and me is real."

Lexie sighed. "I don't have the answer, but if Will loves you, if he really loves you, he'll want you to be happy, even if it's not with him."

Rose was still thinking about Lexie's words as she made her way home from the city in the backseat of the Russells' car. Was it that simple? Could she expect Will to be happy for her even though she'd hurt him? Could she do the same if Bodhi decided he wanted to be with someone else? If someone else made him happier than she did?

She wasn't so sure.

It was almost five when the Russells dropped her off in front of the house. She waved as they drove away, imagining Lexie in the city, surrounded by honking horns and sirens and strangers. The farm was so quiet in comparison, and right then she was glad. Glad that she could see the wind rustle the trees in front of the house, that she could see the herd in the distance, that the only sound she could hear was the tractor as Bodhi made his way up and down the field, turning the long grass into hay.

She shook her head. How could she love a place and want to escape it at the same time?

She walked toward the field where Bodhi was mowing.

Climbing over the fence, she stood at the edge of the field, waving to Bodhi as he worked his way toward her in the tractor. She felt a surge of something powerful and full in her chest as he smiled.

When he came closer, he put the tractor in park and reached for her hand. She laughed as he lifted her up into the cab with him. Settling her on his lap, he put the tractor in gear. They didn't talk. The tractor was too noisy, and they didn't need words anyway. Instead, she put her hands on his face and kissed him full on the lips, drinking him in like it had been nine weeks since she'd seen him instead of nine hours.

The tractor swerved a little, and they both laughed as he set it straight. Then he kissed her back, and she felt the same raw energy that always seemed to be there when they were together.

Like they couldn't get enough of each other. Like it would never be enough.

Forty-One

"Let's see," Rose said, "we've had peach pancakes and peach milk shakes. I think peach cobbler is next."

Bodhi laughed, squeezing her hand. "Only if you're sure we won't explode."

She looked up at him. "Can't handle it?"

"No, I'm good," he said. "Let's do it."

They were at the annual Milford Peach Festival, wandering between booths and sampling everything. August had come in just as hot and dry as July, and Rose alternated between almost-constant worry about the farm and almost-constant bliss. Bodhi had slipped into her life like there had always been a spot waiting for him, an empty place she hadn't even known existed until he'd filled it. She tried to ignore the ticking clock under their time together and focus on the good things, like Marty said. Her dad still wasn't working the farm, but at least he made a show of being social when Maggie came by to drop off one of her desserts, and Buttercup was finally gaining weight.

The sky was darkening when they took their paper bowls of peach cobbler to the field for fireworks.

"Oh, no," Rose said when she saw all the people spread out. "Someone's in our spot."

Bodhi's gaze traveled to the spot by the trees where they'd watched Fourth of July fireworks. "We could sit somewhere else."

Rose seemed to think about it. "We could . . ."

"Actually," Bodhi said, "I have a better idea."

"You do?" she asked.

He nodded. "I think I might have another spot, but it's not here. And there's no guarantee." He laughed. "We might have the best view ever, or we might not be able to see a thing. You game?"

She looked up at him. He was holding her hand. He was really hers. She knew it every time he looked at her. "I'll take my chances."

He took her half-empty bowl and stacked it with his, then dumped them both in a nearby trash.

"Hey!" she protested. "I was still eating that!"

He grinned. "We have to hurry."

Taking her hand, he pulled her along as he jogged toward the parking lot, both of them laughing as they dodged people heading to the field.

He opened her door when they got to the truck and ran

around to the driver's seat.

Rose laughed. "Where are we going?"

"You'll see," he said, firing up the engine.

He navigated the truck past all the traffic heading to the festival and continued down Main Street. They were pulling into the road leading to the farm when Rose realized they were going home.

"You said you had a fireworks spot!"

He glanced over at her. "Just trust me, Rose."

He pulled up in front of the house and ran around to the passenger side of the truck. Opening her door, he helped her out and pulled her toward the barn.

She groaned. "Tell me you're not putting us both to work right now."

He didn't say anything, just led her into the barn and over to the ladder leading to the hayloft.

She crossed her arms over her chest and smiled. "Is this the cowboy equivalent of inviting me to your room to listen to music?"

"Time will tell."

She swatted his leg as he started up the ladder. "Don't want you to go first with a dress on," he said as he climbed.

"What a gentleman," she said.

She followed him up the ladder and into the airless space of the hayloft. She was getting ready to ask what he had in mind when he grabbed a familiar step stool and reached toward the ceiling, pushing on a small square in the metal roof that she'd never noticed before. She watched in awe as the night sky became visible through a hole in the ceiling.

He climbed up and out, then reached down for her hand. "Come on."

She stood on the stool and took his hand, and a moment later she was on the roof of the barn, the fields stretched out in every direction, the house barely visible through the trees. The sky was the perfect color of indigo just before night really descended, a soft exhalation between light and dark.

"I had no idea this was here," Rose said. "How could I not know it was here?"

He shrugged. "I found it a couple of weeks ago one night when I thought I was going to die of heat stroke. I was getting ready to go to the orchard, but when I passed under a certain spot in the ceiling, I felt a draft. I looked up, and there it was." He held her hand as they scooted along the sloping roof to a spot about two feet from the hatch. "If my calculations are correct, this should get us a view of the fireworks."

"Your calculations?" She laughed. "All right, professor."

He smiled, then leaned over to kiss her. "You okay up here? Is this good?"

"Good? It's amazing." She looked at him. "Thank you."

"Don't thank me yet," he said. "Let's make sure we can see something first."

And then, as if on cue, the first burst of color exploded in the air in the distance, directly in front of them. Bodhi put his arm around her shoulders and pulled her close while a second explosion of color—this one gold and white—burst into the air, slowly dissipating in the night sky just before the next one appeared.

It was so quiet without the music that was played at the festival during fireworks. Now there was only the distant pop of fireworks, then the sound of crickets in the tall grass. Rose nestled under Bodhi's arm, wanting to imprint the moment on her mind so she could call on it later. Wanting to remember the weight of his arm on her shoulders, bare under the thin straps of her sundress, the feel of his thigh pressed to hers. Most of all she wanted to remember being up so high, and not being scared at all, because somehow she knew that Bodhi would never let her fall.

She was more aware of him than ever. More aware of his magnetic pull, the soft sound of his breath, his smell of musk and earth and soap. She was dizzy with it, and she held on to him throughout the show, the racing of her heart completely unrelated to the fireworks, to being up on the roof of the barn.

When it was over, they sat in silence for a long time.

"Ready to go back down?" Bodhi finally asked. She wondered why his voice was gruff. Why it seemed to take effort for him to speak.

She nodded when she realized her words weren't coming easily either.

He scooted back toward the hatch in the roof. "I'll go first and help you down."

He swung easily into the hayloft and then held up his arms. "Swing your legs over. I've got you."

She did as he instructed, hesitating at the top of the opening.

"Rose," he said, looking up at her, "I've got you. I promise."

She pushed off from the roof, sliding down into the hay-loft. He put his hands on her waist and she slid the rest of the way, their bodies pressed together as her feet hit the floor.

She didn't step away, and he didn't remove his arms from around her waist. They were both breathing hard, their eyes locked as tightly together as their bodies. There was a current running between them, like the charge in the air just before lightning cracked the sky.

Then all at once, his mouth was on hers, their kisses hungry, their hands roaming each other's bodies. Rose broke away, stepping back a little and pulling her dress over her head. She tossed it aside without taking her eyes off him. She stood in front of him in nothing but her bra and underwear, the warm air of the barn lighting on her bare skin as gently as Bodhi's hand when he reached up to caress her face.

"Are you sure?"

She nodded. "I'm sure."

And she was. She'd never been more sure of anything in her life.

She stepped toward him, wanting him to believe it, and wrapped her arms around his neck. He stared at her for a long minute, and she knew then, knew how he felt about her, that this meant everything to him that it did to her.

He scooped her up in his arms and carried her across

the loft, setting her gently down on the mattress that lay on the floor amid the hay. He touched her face carefully, like he wanted to be sure she was real, before lowering his mouth to hers.

And then there was nothing but the two of them and the soft light of the barn and the stars overhead through the open hatch and the certainty that they belonged to each other.

Forty-Two

Bodhi walked down the rows of cut hay, inspecting it for mold or damp that could lead to mold, and turning it over with the pitchfork in his hand when it seemed necessary. The lack of rain was their friend when it came to putting up hay, but it was still wreaking havoc on their supply.

The thought didn't worry him as much as it should have. He was too busy replaying the night before in his mind. Too busy thinking about Rose, the feel of her in his arms, her head on his bare chest, her hair flowing out around them.

Every experience he'd had with a girl looked cheap compared to the things he'd shared with Rose. It didn't matter whether they were riding, walking the fields, swimming in the pond, making dinner together. Everything with her was sacred.

She was good and smart and pure and strong. She'd had

tradition and family and love to shape her where he'd had only uncertainty and solitude. But somehow they fit, and for the first time in his life, Bodhi thought he might even deserve something good. Someone good. Someone like Rose. The Bodhi he'd been before seemed like a distant memory. He was different with her. Stronger and better. Maybe even good, like her.

She'd slipped from the barn just before midnight, and he'd gotten up and opened his computer, buying her a plane ticket to Edinburgh on his flight without a second thought. By the light of day, it seemed an impulsive thing to do, but it was done now, and he was both nervous and excited to ask her to go with him. He was already thinking ahead, planning the moment, wanting it to be a new beginning for them both.

He thought she might regret what had happened between them, but she'd reappeared in the barn at four a.m., just like any other day. He'd been nervous, waiting for her to give him a clue how she felt about everything, but she'd come right to him, wrapping her arms around his neck and kissing him in a way that made it clear she had no regrets.

He looked up from the fields and saw her standing by the fence. She was like that. She seemed to change the air around her so that he almost always knew when she was around. She waved, beaming, and signaled that it was time for lunch. He held up the fingers on one hand to let her know he needed five more minutes.

She disappeared into the house and Bodhi continued down the line, turning at the end of the row.

He set the pitchfork next to the barn and went into the bathroom to wash up. Then he changed his shirt and headed for the house. He was halfway across the path separating the house from the barn when he saw the man walking up the driveway.

He stopped, wondering who it could be on a Sunday afternoon. But a moment later something about the man caught Bodhi's attention—the lazy gait, the tip of his head under his hat, the obstinate set of his shoulders—and then Bodhi knew.

He waited, the blood rushing through his veins like a freight train until the man stopped right in front of him.

"Well, well, well. In New York after all," the man said. "Can't hardly believe it."

Bodhi crossed his arms over his chest. "What are you doing here?"

"Well, now, I just come to say hello to my only son," he said. "Can't a man do that anymore?"

He remembered his father as tall and lean, imposing, with taut wiry muscle that Bodhi had experienced first-hand. The man in front of him was diminished. Still tall, but skinny in a way that made it clear he hadn't done any heavy lifting in a long, long time. Teeth that had once been white and straight were now slightly yellowed, and he was missing a couple near the front of his mouth.

This was not someone Bodhi would normally be afraid of. But he was afraid now. Afraid that he would suddenly go back to being the scared little kid who'd had no choice but to run, who'd felt safer sleeping in abandoned barns and being alone in the world than he'd felt with his father. Most of all he was afraid for Rose. He didn't want his father anywhere near her.

"You're not my father," Bodhi said, arms still crossed.

His dad laughed, then coughed at the end of it, a wet, barking sound that seemed to come from deep in his lungs. "That's just not true, son. I'm your daddy whether you like it or not."

"I don't," Bodhi said. "And I say you're not. So why don't you just tell me what you're doing here."

A mean light flashed in his dad's eyes. "Can't even invite a man inside after such a long trip?"

"No."

He sighed, rubbing the gray hair that grew patchy and thin at his jawline. "Well, the truth is, son, I'm in a bit of trouble."

"What a surprise."

"Now don't be like that," his dad said. "Everyone needs help from time to time."

Bodhi didn't want to name the sadness that rose in him at his father's words. "I needed help, too. And I didn't get it from you."

"I did the best I could, son. Sure enough, I made mistakes, but every man does."

"I'm not going to stand here and argue the validity of your mistakes," Bodhi said. "Just tell me what you want and go."

"I'm not going to stand here and argue the validity of your mistakes," his dad mocked, his voice high and full of scorn. "Sounds like maybe you've gotten a little big for your britches."

Bodhi uncrossed his arms. "I'm going inside. You better be off this property before I come back out here."

"I need some money, son," his dad said to his back.

Bodhi turned around. "I'm not giving you any money. Don't have it anyway."

"I'm not sure I believe that," his dad said. "Been working all this time, moving around. Must have some money stashed somewhere."

"I don't."

His dad turned his gaze to the Darrows' farmhouse, and Bodhi suddenly saw it through his eyes; the wide front porch, the sturdy wicker furniture, the heavy double-glazed windows.

"Seems like you might be able to get a little advance from your employers for a family member in need."

Bodhi was still looking at the house when Rose stepped onto the porch in shorts and a T-shirt, her hair tied back in a loose ponytail.

"Bodhi?" she called out. "Who is that?"

His dad chuckled under his breath. "Bodhi. What kind of name is that? The name your mom and I gave you not good enough for you now?"

"Nobody," he called, waving her back inside. "I'll be right there."

She hesitated, then came down the walkway. Bodhi watched her approach with dread, but he knew he couldn't stop her. Rose wasn't the kind of girl who took orders, and while he loved that about her, just this once he wished she'd listen.

She stood next to Bodhi and looked at his father. "Hello. What can we do for you?"

"Just came by to say hello," his father said, flashing Rose a toothy grin. He held out his hand. "I'm Roger's father."

Confusion swept over Rose's features. "Roger . . . ?"

"That's right," his dad said, "you don't know him by his given name. I guess you call him Bodhi."

She looked at Bodhi then, and he knew she was remembering all the things he'd told her about his past. She spoke his name softly, the first traces of concern showing in her eyes. "Bodhi?"

"It's okay," he said, careful to keep his voice steady. "Go inside. I've got this under control."

She hesitated, then nodded and started back for the house.

"Nice to meet you," his dad called after her.

She didn't respond, and Bodhi knew from the set of her shoulders that she was angry. "Little bitch," his dad muttered under his breath.

Bodhi wasn't even aware of charging him until he felt the fabric of his father's shirt in his hands. "Don't you ever talk about her again. Don't even look at her."

His dad surprised him by laughing, following it up with another wheezy cough. "Think I've touched a nerve. Is my boy in love?"

Bodhi shoved him away, and he staggered back before finding his footing.

"Get out of here," Bodhi said. "And don't ever try to find me again. You're dead to me."

He turned and walked toward the house, half afraid his dad would follow, or just as bad, that he'd stand out in front of the house until Bodhi gave him what he wanted. But when he stepped onto the porch and opened the screen door, his father was already making his way back down the drive to the road.

Forty-Three

Rose watched from the living room window with her heart in her throat. That was the man who had raised Bodhi, who had hurt him. And now he was here. What could he possibly want?

She jumped a little when Bodhi charged him, then reached for her phone. There was a police station in town. The force itself was small, but they could probably be on the farm in less than five minutes.

But a minute later Bodhi let his father go. Rose watched as he staggered backward. They exchanged a few more words, and then Bodhi was heading up the walkway to the house.

She met him in the foyer, waiting until he'd shut the door behind him to speak. "Are you okay?"

"Fine." He said the word, but she knew that he was anything but fine. His face was two shades paler than normal, his jaw set like he was gritting his teeth.

She wrapped her arms around him, waiting until his own arms came around her shoulders. They stood like that for a minute until Rose stepped away. "Come on."

She took his hand and led him back to the kitchen where she poured him a glass of cold water from the pitcher they kept in the fridge. She leaned against the counter while he drank, giving him time to get his bearings.

"Now," she said, "are you okay?"

He set down his glass and rubbed his jaw. "I'm all right." He hesitated. "I just don't like that he came here, that's all."

The look on his face—a vulnerability he wouldn't want to know she saw—caused a gust of anger to rise in her. She turned around, pulling dishes down from the cabinets for lunch and setting them down on the counter a little too hard. A moment later she felt his hands on her shoulders.

"Rose."

She turned around and looked up at him. "I could kill him."

He pushed a strand of hair away from her face. "Don't worry. He won't be back."

She shook her head. "Not because he came here. Because of what he did to you. I don't think I've ever hated someone until today."

He held her face between his hands. "Don't be mad on my account. Any wounds I had were healed the minute I found you." He bent his head to kiss her.

She kissed him back, but she wondered if he even knew it wasn't true. Some wounds never healed. They turned into scars. You got used to the look of them, the feel of them under your fingers. They became a part of you. Maybe you wouldn't even feel like yourself without them.

"Smells good." Her father's voice made her jump a little, and Bodhi put three feet between them in under five seconds. She thought her dad might say something about the position he'd caught them in, but he just looked from one of them to the other. "Everything okay?"

She glanced at Bodhi, willing him to stay silent about his father. That's the last thing her dad needed to worry about right now.

"Everything's fine, Dad," she said before Bodhi could speak. "I made pot roast. You eating with us?"

He wandered over to the stove, sniffing at the big pan she'd taken out of the oven. "Smells like your mother's."

"It is. It's from her cookbook." She went to the table and pulled out a chair for him. "Sit, Daddy. I'll get you something to drink."

She was acting weird, talking too fast and moving around the kitchen like a bird trapped inside, all in an effort to distract her dad from the possibility that something was wrong.

He sat down slowly, and she went to work pouring drinks and getting food on the table while Bodhi talked to her dad about the quality of this year's hay. She didn't want to think about the man who had come here, the man who called himself Bodhi's father. Bodhi said he wouldn't come back. She trusted him, but she still had to fight against the feeling that the perfect world they'd built had somehow been compromised.

Forty-Four

She was leaning against the fence two days later, kissing Bodhi as the cows milled in the distance, when she heard boots on the gravel behind her. She turned in Bodhi's arms, half expecting to see Bodhi's father coming up the drive.

It was Will.

"Hey," she said, stepping away from Bodhi.

"Hey."

They hadn't spoken once since their fight in the Breiners' barn. She'd hoped time would repair the rift between them, but she could tell from the set of his shoulders, the flinty expression on his face, that nothing had changed. Sadness swept through her as she walked toward him. Where was the Will she knew? The one whose easy smile and carefree laugh had gotten her through so many hard days?

"What's up?" she asked when they were a few feet apart.

"Dad sent me over with some milk." He shrugged a little to indicate the gallon of milk in either hand.

"Thank you." She reached out, and he handed her the plastic containers.

He looked past her at Bodhi, still leaning against the fence where she'd left him.

"Will," Bodhi said.

Will gave the smallest of nods before turning his attention back to Rose.

"Want to come in for some lemonade or something?" she asked him.

He shook his head. "Got to get back." He turned to leave.

"I miss you, Will," she said softly.

He looked at her. "Don't, Rose. Just don't."

She watched as he continued down the path, crossed the dirt road, and hopped over the orchard fence. A minute later, she felt Bodhi's hands on her shoulders.

"I'm sorry," he said. "Not about us. Never that. But sorry about the way things are with Will."

She shook her head. "It's not your fault."

"Want me to talk to him?" Bodhi asked.

"No, that'll just make it worse. He'll come around. He'll have to."

Bodhi turned her around to face him. "You know what?"

"What?"

"I'm going to take you to dinner," Bodhi said. "And your dad, too, if he'll come."

Rose smiled. "You don't have to do that."

"I want to. We'll go to Clementine's and have some of Marie's triple chocolate fudge cake for dessert. Didn't you tell me chocolate makes everything better when we ate those cherries?"

She laughed. "You win. Let me run in and see if my dad wants to come."

She hurried into the house, stopping in her room to change into something nicer than her shorts and tank top, then continued down the hall to her dad's room. He was sitting on the bed, staring at the open window, the curtain moving in the barely there breeze that came in through the window.

"Daddy?"

He turned his head to look at her. "Hi, honey. Something the matter?"

"No. I was just coming to see if you wanted to go into town with Bodhi and me for dinner. We're going to Clementine's."

"Oh, I don't think so, honey. I'm going to chip away at some of those casseroles in the freezer."

She stepped into the room and sat on the edge of the bed. "What were you doing just now, Dad?"

He looked confused. "What do you mean?"

"When I came in. You were looking at the window."

He glanced back at it, like that might somehow shake loose the memory he needed. "I don't know, really. Sometimes I just sit and think. I guess that's what I was doing."

"What were you thinking about?" she asked.

He looked right at her then, his eyes clearer than they'd

been in a while. "I was thinking about your mother."

Rose smiled a little. It still hurt to think of her mother, but sometime over the past couple of months the vise on her heart had gradually loosened. "What about her?"

He hesitated. "I was remembering. Back when we were kids." He paused, but she waited, hoping he would go on. A few seconds later, he did. "We used to go to the pond on evenings like this one. We'd swim until it cooled off, then climb into the branches of the apple trees where we could feel the breeze better. Sometimes we'd stay there until your grandpa started hollering for her to come to dinner."

"That sounds nice." Rose could see them, young and falling in love.

He nodded. "It was." His gaze seemed to clear. "What about you? Are you doing okay, honey?"

She nodded. "I'm good."

"You and Bodhi seem to have gotten . . . close." His voice was gruff, and she willed herself not to blush. "And I hear there's some kind of rift between you and Will. Are the two things related?"

She didn't know what to make of the question. After months of minimal conversation, was this her dad trying to be involved? Trying to brush up on what was going on in her life?

"A little," she admitted.

He seemed to think for a minute before reaching over to pat her hand. "You don't owe anything to anybody but yourself. Remember that."

Forty-Five

"I think you have a secret plot to make me fat," Bodhi groaned, leaning back in his chair.

Clementine's was busy, and they'd chosen a table outside on the sidewalk before ordering giant hamburgers with French fries and three big slices of cake, one of them to go for Rose's dad.

Rose laughed. "You invited me to dinner!"

"True, but you decided on the hamburger."

"That doesn't mean you had to order it."

"I might not have if you'd warned me that it was a pound of beef."

She rolled her eyes. "That was not a pound. You're exaggerating. Besides, I'm starting to see a pattern here."

"What do you mean?" he asked

"First the food at the peach festival and now this. Just

admit it; I can eat more than you!"

"I want to argue the point," he said, "but I'm too full."

"Ha! I knew it!"

He grinned from across the table, then held her eyes.

"What?" she said.

"I just don't think I've ever been this happy," he said. "And I know I've never smiled as much. Maybe not in my whole life."

Her heart squeezed with melancholy. "I'm glad."

"Ready?" he asked. "If we leave now, we might be able to catch the sunset from the orchard."

"Sounds perfect."

They said goodbye to Marie on their way out, then got in the truck and headed home.

They parked in front of the house, and Bodhi walked around to open her door, something he insisted on even after she had told him it was silly.

"Let's take this inside to my dad," she said. "Then we can walk over to the orchard."

They were almost to the porch when they heard the sound of shattering glass from inside. They looked at each other in the split second before they started running.

Bodhi threw open the screen door. "Stay behind me," he said.

They crept into the foyer, glancing at the living room. It had been ransacked: cushions pulled off the sofa, the TV tipped over onto the floor, all of the knickknacks and pictures and books pulled off the shelves.

Bodhi turned to her. "Go outside and call the police. Right now."

"My dad's in here! There's no way I'm going outside!"

She saw the conflict on his face, knew he wanted to press the issue but also didn't want to stand there arguing about it when someone was breaking into the house.

"Stay back," he said, already moving forward.

Pictures had been knocked off the hallway wall, and Rose could see even as they rounded the corner into the kitchen that it was a mess, too. Rose recognized the floral border of her mother's china in some of the porcelain littering the floor. The drawers were all open, their contents spilling out onto the floor.

A man stood with his back to them near the old hutch by the kitchen table. He was muttering to himself as he shoved a set of old silver candlesticks into a backpack.

Before Rose knew what was happening, Bodhi had launched himself at the man. Just before Bodhi reached him, the man turned, and Rose saw that it was Bodhi's father.

They went down, shattered glass crunching under their bodies as Bodhi rolled on top of him. Then Bodhi was punching and punching, his back flexing as he lifted his arm again and again, brought it down again and again.

"Bodhi, no! Stop it!" She was screaming at him. Not because she cared what happened to the man who had broken into her house, who had once hurt the person she loved, but because she didn't recognize Bodhi's face with the mask of rage covering his normally serene features. Nothing scared her more until she remembered her father.

"Dad?" she called out, heading for the door of the kitchen. "Where are you, Dad?"

She heard a muffled groan from behind the kitchen island and followed the sound across the room. Her father lay on the tile floor, his head bleeding profusely, his face a mess of cuts and bruises that were already turning purple.

"Daddy!"

She cradled his head in her lap, and then Bodhi was there, right next to her. Glancing across the room, she saw that his father was still, his eyes closed. She wondered if he was dead and was surprised to find that she didn't care.

"Rose . . . Rose!" She heard Bodhi calling her name through a haze of shock. When she turned to look at him, he met her eyes, his expression calm. "I'm calling an ambulance, Rose. Everything's going to be okay."

Forty-Six

Bodhi finished giving his statement to the police and then went to find Rose. When he didn't find her in the emergency room lobby, he went to the greeter's desk at the front of the room.

"May I help you?" The woman was about Maggie Ryland's age, with gray hair that curled near her ears and pink-rimmed glasses edged in rhinestones.

"I'm looking for an update on John Darrow," Bodhi said. "He was brought in about an hour ago."

Her smile was warm. "Are you immediate family?"

"No. Just a . . . a friend." He felt traitorous saying it. He couldn't call himself a friend of John Darrow's after what his father had done.

"I'm sorry," she said. "We can't give out patient information unless you're an immediate family member."

He nodded, patting the Formica desk between them, trying to quell his frustration. Retreating to the waiting room, he took a chair in the corner and dropped his head into his hands.

This was his fault. He hadn't been around his dad in years, but Bodhi should have known he wouldn't leave quietly. Not after his father had seen the Darrows' house and property. Not when he needed money.

Bodhi and Rose had waited in silence until the police and ambulance arrived. John had been semiconscious, at least. That was a good sign. The same couldn't be said of Bodhi's father, although Bodhi couldn't have cared less about that. According to the police, his father was alive and would be extradited back to Colorado where there was an active warrant for his arrest. It was too good a punishment for him as far as Bodhi was concerned.

Self-loathing had seeped into every crevice of his body since they'd arrived at the hospital. Rose had gone with her father while Bodhi talked to the police. Normally he'd be nervous talking to the law, not because he'd ever done anything wrong but because he'd spent so much time trying to stay out of sight. He had to remind himself that he was almost nineteen. He could go anywhere now, and the police, locals who knew the Darrow family well, hadn't had anything but compliments for the way Bodhi had handled the situation.

But he had done this, as sure as if he'd done it himself. He had brought all the ugliness of his past to the one place—to the two people—who least deserved it. He'd been trying to find the right time to give Rose the plane ticket, to ask her to come with him. He knew she wouldn't want to leave her dad, but he also had a feeling she might be looking for a way out. The farm was struggling under the weight of the drought. The Darrows couldn't afford to hire someone new for fall, which meant Rose would be right back where she'd been at the beginning of the summer, doing everything herself. She deserved better, and he'd been a little giddy at the idea of making an escape together, getting on a plane and leaving all the sadness and loss behind.

Now he knew it was a fairy tale. He'd gotten carried away. Had forgotten who he really was, where he came from. Had deluded himself into thinking it didn't matter in the face of his feelings for Rose. All lies. How could he stay in Rose's life after this? How could she trust him? How could her father trust him?

"There you are!" Rose's voice interrupted his thoughts, and he turned to find her rushing toward him. "I've been trying to text you." Marty trailed a few steps behind.

Right. Marty. One more person to disappoint.

He stood. "I left my phone at home. The front desk wouldn't tell me anything."

His arms opened for her automatically, and she stepped into them and leaned her head on his chest. "Are you okay?"

"Don't worry about me." He could barely choke the words out. "How's your dad?"

"He'll be all right," Rose said. "They think he might have a minor concussion, but other than that, he's stable. They're going to keep him overnight just to be safe."

He nodded. "I'm glad."

She raised her head and stepped away from him. "Tell me about your dad."

"Nothing to tell," he said. "They're sending him back to Colorado to face charges there. He won't be able to bother you anymore."

"Us," Rose said. "He won't be able to bother *us*."

Bodhi gave her a tight nod.

He felt a light touch on his shoulder and realized Marty was standing next to him, her green eyes piercing his. "This wasn't your fault," she said softly. "End of story."

It wasn't true, but it wasn't Marty's job to make him feel better, and he knew if he argued the point that's exactly what she'd try to do.

"I'm going to make sure they have your dad's insurance information," Marty said to Rose. "I'll be right back."

Rose nodded, her hand still on Bodhi's waist, like she was afraid he'd vanish if she stopped touching him. She waited for Marty to disappear around a corner before turning back to Bodhi.

"You do know this isn't your fault, don't you?" she asked softly.

He looked past her, over her shoulder. He could give her what she wanted, say the things she wanted to hear. But he'd lied to her enough. About his plans at the end of the summer, and most of all about himself. About who he was and what he could offer her.

"Bodhi?" A note of fear had crept into her voice.

He swallowed hard and forced himself to look down at her. He wouldn't be a coward, at least. "This is a bad idea, Rose. I've always known it. I just didn't want to believe it."

She shook her head. "What are you saying?"

"I can't give you . . . anything," he said. "And you deserve . . . everything."

"You *do* give me everything," she said, panic in her eyes. "Everything that matters."

"It's not true, Rose. You want it to be true. So do I." He hesitated, knowing once he said the rest of it there would be no going back. They wouldn't belong to each other anymore. "But it's not, and it's better if we end this now."

"Don't do this," she said.

It took every ounce of strength in his body to step away from her. "Someone has to." He took a long look at her. He would finish his job on the farm, especially now that John Darrow was injured. But this was the last time he'd see her like this. Like she was still his. "I'm sorry, Rose."

And then he turned and walked away, before he could be selfish and change his mind.

Forty-Seven

Rose was still sitting on the chair in the lobby when her aunt found her twenty minutes later.

"You'd think with the price of medical care here they could at least . . ." She trailed off. "Rose? Honey?"

Rose looked up at her. "He's gone."

Marty took the chair next to her. "What do you mean, 'He's gone'? Bodhi's leaving the farm?"

Rose shrugged. "I don't know. I don't . . . I don't think he'd do that to us. Not until the hay is put up. Especially not now, with Dad . . ."

Marty put her arm around Rose shoulders. "Then tell me what you're saying."

"He thinks this is his fault. He said . . ." She choked back a sob. "He said we were a bad idea, that he couldn't give me anything."

MICHELLE ZINK

Marty rubbed her back, and Rose had a flash of memory, her mother doing the very same thing when Rose had the flu in ninth grade. "He's just upset, honey. He'll come around."

"I don't think so, Aunt Marty. I think he's always felt this way—like he wasn't good enough—and now he has an excuse to believe it."

Marty took a deep breath, like she was just realizing something important. "Do you really believe that?"

"I believe he believes it," Rose said.

Marty didn't say anything for a minute. When she finally did speak, there was a note of certainty in her voice that Rose recognized. It was the voice Marty used when she was completely sure of something, when she'd finally figured something out.

"Then you have to go," she said. "Tell him he's wrong."

Rose shook her head. "He won't listen."

"Are you going to let that stop you?" Marty asked.

"I don't . . . If he won't . . ."

Marty took her hand. "You have to try. Go now, before he's had time to convince himself he did the right thing."

"What about Dad?"

"They gave him something to help him sleep. He'll be fine, and I'll stay for a bit. He would want you to do this." She met Rose's eyes. "If he were himself, he would want you to do this, and so would your mother."

Her mother. Rose thought about her passion and her backbone. She would never let someone she loved walk away. Not without a fight.

She leaned in to give her aunt a hug. "Thanks, Marty."

She hurried out the big sliding doors at the front of the emergency room. By the time she hit the sidewalk she was running.

It was almost midnight when she parked in front of the house. She had no idea how Bodhi had gotten home, but she said a silent prayer of thanks that he'd thought to follow the ambulance in the truck. Otherwise she would have had to call a cab, and they weren't exactly easy to find in the areas around Milford.

The farm was silent, a full moon rising up over the barn. The police had still been here when they left, but now the windows in the house were dark, the driveway in front empty except for the Ford Taurus her dad sometimes drove.

She didn't have the heart to face the wreckage inside, or even to think about all the things that had been destroyed. Besides, that's not why she was here.

She went straight to the barn, opening the doors as quietly as she could so she wouldn't startle the animals, or Bodhi if he was sleeping. She thought about Marty's question, about whether Bodhi was leaving the farm, and panic swelled inside her. What if she was wrong and he was already gone?

Hurrying to the hayloft, she climbed the ladder, her heart in her throat. The loft came into view a little at a time, and then she was at the top and he was there, lying in bed with his back to her, his shoulders bare over the sheet around his waist.

She was quiet when she stepped into the loft, but it was

impossible to be totally silent. He had to know she was there. She paused. There was so much she wanted to say. So much she wanted to tell him. But all of those things, all of those words, weren't the most important thing between them. There was something else, a bone-deep affinity that had taken her by surprise, growing and growing until she realized it had been there all along, wrapped tight inside itself like a tiny seedling. That's why she'd been scared of him in the first place. She knew that now.

She stepped closer to the bed, her footsteps ringing out on the wood floor. Bodhi's back was rising and falling too quickly, his breath a match to the racing of her heart.

She pulled off her boots and drew her sundress over her head. Reaching behind her, she removed the tie from the end of her braid and undid her hair until it fell in loose waves around her bare shoulders. Slipping under the covers, she stretched her body against Bodhi's bare back, sliding an arm around his waist, before she could change her mind. They lay like that for a few minutes before she dared to speak.

"Will you look at me?"

At first she thought he hadn't heard her, that he really was asleep. But then he turned in her arms so that their faces were only a few inches apart.

She reached up, put her hands on his face, and looked into his eyes. "It's too late. Only your leaving can hurt me now."

"Rose . . ."

She lifted herself up on one elbow, her hair falling around

them, blocking out the rest of the world. "The truth?"

"Always," he said, his voice hoarse.

She smiled. "I love you, Bodhi Lowell. Stop pretending either of us will be okay without the other one."

For a few seconds, she thought he might argue the point. But a moment later a soft sigh escaped his lips, and he pulled her head to his chest.

"I love you, Rose. So much. And I'm going to do everything I can to prove that to you as long as you'll let me."

She kissed the bare skin on his chest and worked her way up his neck, pausing over his mouth. "You'll stay, then?"

She thought she saw hesitation in his eyes, but then he nodded and his mouth was on hers and she forgot about everything but him.

Forty-Eight

They spent the next morning cleaning up the mess in the house. Marty was bringing John Darrow home in the afternoon, and Bodhi wanted to make sure everything was ready before he got there. He felt physically ill as they swept the broken shards of china that had belonged to Rose's mother, as they picked old photographs off the floor, pulling out the broken glass and rehanging them until they could replace the frames. There were times he wanted to run, escape to the barn to avoid facing what his father had done, but he forced himself to help Rose, to clean the blood on the floor where his father had beat up Rose's dad. It was the only penance he could do for now.

Rose didn't say a word. He knew she was hurt by all the damage—almost everything in the Darrow home was old, handed down from one relative or another—but he also knew she would never let him see it. She was protecting him, even while he wanted to protect her.

He thought about the plane ticket he'd bought for her. Today he would make things right with Marty and John Darrow. Then he would ask Rose to come to Europe with him. They would wear backpacks and squish together in twin beds in cheap hostels. They would try food they'd never heard of and take corny pictures together. They would leave behind their sadness and loss until they could both come back whole.

He would stay with her like he'd promised. Just not here.

Rose looked around the living room and straightened one last pillow. "I think that's about it."

"It looks good," Bodhi said. "And I'm going to replace all of those broken frames."

She slid an arm around his waist. "Don't be silly. Who needs glass in a picture frame anyway?"

"But all that stuff . . ." He looked down at the two trash bags by their feet. "It meant something to you."

She hesitated a little before nodding. "I won't lie and say that it didn't. But it doesn't mean as much to me as my dad does, or you. Nowhere close. And you know what? I'm starting to think we sometimes have to lose things to remember what really matters."

He kissed the top of her head. "You're amazing, Rose Darrow. Has anyone ever told you that?"

She looked up at him, fluttering her eyelashes dramatically. "Once or twice."

He swatted her bottom playfully. "I'm going to head to the barn."

"But my dad will be home soon! You have to say hello."

"I'll be back, but I think you should get him settled first."

"Okay," she said.

He bent his head and touched his lips to hers. "I love you."

She smiled. "I still can't believe it's real when you say that."

"Believe it. Nothing's ever been more true."

He stepped away, holding her hand until distance made it impossible to hold it any longer.

"See you later," Rose said.

He nodded. "You will."

He left through the front door and made his way across the drive to the barn. When he got there, he took a quick shower in the bathroom next to the bunk room and headed for the loft in his towel. He was crossing the room to the plastic bin that held his clean clothes when he stopped, his feet suddenly frozen to the ground.

The air felt charged with presence, like someone had just been there. He wasn't afraid. There was nowhere to hide, and besides, who would be in his room now that his father was behind bars? But he walked slowly into the room any-way, really looking at everything, trying to figure out what had changed.

He checked his pack first—everything was there—and then moved on to his clothes and the money he kept stashed in an old coffee can. Everything was where it should be, but he still couldn't shake the feeling that the space had been inexorably altered.

He changed into clean clothes, still fighting the sensation that someone else had been in the loft. Pacing the floor a few times, he finally opened up his computer, looking for a distraction until he could be sure Rose's dad was home and settled. The first thing he did was change his email address. He didn't want reminders of the past. No more thinking about his father and where he was and what he was doing. He wished Christine and all the people he'd met along the way well, but he was going to start fresh, and he was going to do it with Rose Darrow. He'd been stupid to think he could leave her behind, to think that his words would separate them. They would always belong to each other, whatever he said.

He pulled up some of the hostels he'd bookmarked for his trip, double-checking to make sure they were good enough for Rose. She wouldn't care, but he didn't want her staying in some flea-ridden dump. When he was satisfied that cheap didn't necessarily mean dirty, he sat back in the chair, his stomach clenching.

What if she said no? He hadn't let himself think about it, but there was no guarantee she'd want to go with him. She'd worry about her dad—that was for sure—but he'd tell her she deserved this. That she deserved to live for herself now. Still, there was no way to be sure she'd agree.

Shutting the computer, he jumped up from the chair

and wiped his palms on his jeans. What he had to do next wouldn't be easy, but it seemed like nothing right ever was. Nothing but Rose. Loving her was the one easy, simple thing he'd ever done.

Marty's car was still out front when he made his way up the walkway to the house. When he got to the front door, he took a deep breath and rapped on the wood frame of the screen.

Rose's face appeared on the other side a moment later. She opened the door and smiled. "I thought you'd finally gotten used to coming in without knocking."

"This isn't a social call," he said.

She scowled a little. "What do you mean? What's going on?"

"I'd like to speak to your father."

She opened the door wider. "Come in."

He nodded and stepped through the door, then followed Rose down the hall to the living room. She looked back at him nervously, and he smiled to try and ease her mind.

Marty was curled up on one end of the couch. Rose's dad sat on the other. A bandage covered half his forehead, and one eye was swollen and purple. He started to rise when Bodhi came into the room.

"Please, sir," Bodhi said, holding up both hands. "No need to get up."

John eased himself back onto the couch with the slow movements of a man whose whole body hurt.

"Have a seat, Bodhi," Marty said.

Bodhi shook his head. "I'll stand while I say what I have to say, but thank you."

"Okay, then," she said.

Bodhi wiped his sweaty palms on his jeans and looked at John Darrow. "I came to apologize, sir. I—" John started to interrupt him, but he continued. "Please. I just . . . I need to say this."

John nodded.

"I know you'll say it wasn't my fault, that I'm not responsible for the things my dad did, but he came here a couple of days ago, and the truth is, I should have known something like this might happen." He looked down at his boots. "He's not . . . well, he's not a good man. Not like you." He forced himself to look up at Rose's dad. "I should have said something to you or to the police so you could keep an eye out. You've been nothing but good to me, you and Rose and Marty." He let his gaze slide to Marty before looking back at John. "I promise that your faith in me isn't misplaced. I'll never let anything bad happen here again. I hope you can both forgive me."

For a minute, no one said anything. Then John slowly got to his feet and held out his hand. Bodhi took it.

"Son, no man is responsible for another man's actions. That you're willing to take responsibility for not saying anything means a lot, but that's as far as your part in it goes." John gave his hand a shake, then clapped him gently on the shoulder. "I never did hold to the belief that the apple doesn't fall far from the tree. It's been my experience that every man has more than one chance to turn things around for himself. From what I can see, you've done a fine job of it. Any man would be proud to call you their son."

Bodhi blinked back the sting of tears. "Thank you, sir. That means a lot to me."

Marty stood, crossing the small distance between them and wrapping Bodhi in a hug.

"All is well," she said in his ear. "You're doing just fine." She stepped back and looked at him with a smile. "Now sit down, will you?"

They all laughed as Rose's hand slid into his.

Forty-Nine

Rose stopped on her way to the barn, looking out across the field where Bodhi was running the baler, picking up all the loose hay and turning it into the rectangular bales that could be put up by one or two people. She couldn't help smiling, even though he probably wasn't watching her.

She could tell that her dad had been impressed by Bodhi last night, by the fact that Bodhi had apologized to him man-to-man. She still didn't know what was in the cards for them long term, but Bodhi had said he would stay. For the first time, she had faith that they would find a way to make it work. They belonged together. That was all that mattered. Everything else could be figured out.

She continued to the barn, planning to take Raven for a run to the pond. Throwing open the door, she stepped inside and started down the row. Coco stared at her as she approached, snuffling a little when Rose came close.

"Hey, girl," she said, reaching into her pocket for an apple. "Want to try one of these today?"

Coco sniffed at the fruit, then lifted her head in a gesture of disdain. Hesitating, Rose lifted her arms up over the stanchion door and smoothed the hair between Coco's eyes. "Beautiful, strong girl . . . Such a beautiful, strong girl."

The horse whinnied a little, and Rose looked into her eyes, wondering if she still remembered Rose's mother. If she was aware of the loss in a tangible way. If the horse could remember the way her mother spoke or felt on her back, or if the loss was visceral, a feeling rather than knowledge. Would that be better? Would it make it easier?

Rose walked to the wall behind her and took a lead off one of the hooks. Then she lifted the latch on the door, and stepped inside.

At first, Coco was nervous around her, sidestepping and chuffing like she wasn't sure what was going on. But Rose moved slowly, stroking the horse's neck and repeating her mother's words until the animal calmed down.

She led Coco to the tack room and saddled her, then brought her outside. Rose eased her body over the animal's flank, then sat still, giving Coco time to adjust to the weight on her back. When Rose was sure the animal was comfortable, she eased up on the reins and gave her tongue a click.

The horse ambled forward, slowly at first, and then a little faster so that Rose had to rein her in to keep her from breaking into a run. Rose guided her to the field at the back of the house before giving her enough lead to break into a gallop. The horse took off like a shot, and Rose gave her yet more lead, letting her run around the field, feeling the horse's powerful muscles flexing under her thighs. The summer wind loosened some of the hair in Rose's braid, and she laughed out loud as it whipped around her face.

She let Coco wear herself out, slowing down to a canter and then a trot, before leading her across the dirt road to the orchard. They made their way through the trees, heavy with fruit, the apples still small and ripening, the deep mauve of the peaches covered in soft fuzz. She could feel her mother's presence, could hear her whisper.

Beautiful, strong girl . . . Such a beautiful, strong girl.

She was smiling as they ascended the hill leading to the pond. She would give Coco time to stop and drink. Then they would return to the farm and she'd see if Bodhi wanted to come back with her for an evening swim. He would hold her, his body slick against hers. His mouth would taste like the hay he chewed when he drove the tractor, and like the water that bubbled up from a spring under the pond.

But when she got to the top of the hill, she saw that someone else was already there.

Will.

He sat on the bank with his back to her, his hat next to him on the grass. She stopped Coco's progress. She didn't want to fight with Will. But not speaking to each other was just as bad. Maybe he'd calmed down now that some time had passed. Maybe they could work it out.

She nudged Coco into motion, and the horse picked her way down the hill. Will didn't look at her, not when she tied Coco to a tree by the water or when she lowered herself to the grass next to him.

"Hey," she finally said.

"Hello."

She leaned forward. "You can't look at me now? What's with that?"

He pulled some grass from the ground and shook his head. "I don't want to fight. And I don't want to hurt you."

"The only thing that hurts is that you can't be happy for me," she said. "That you can't be happy that I'm happy."

"So you're still together?" Will asked. "You and Bodhi?"

She nodded. "More than ever. And I don't say that to hurt you, but because I want you to understand. I love you, Will. You are like family to me, just like you said. But I'm in love with Bodhi, and he's in love with me, and if you can't be okay with that . . ." She took a deep breath. "Well, I just don't know how it will work."

"Summer's almost over," Will said. "What then?"

Rose shrugged. "I don't know. But we're going to figure something out."

Will turned his face to her, and Rose was startled by the look in his eyes. Not anger like she'd expected, but something else. Something like regret. "That what he said?"

"We haven't talked about the details," Rose admitted. "Not yet. But I know we will."

Will laughed a mean little laugh, then looked out over the water.

"What?" Rose braced herself for another fight, for more of Will's accusations. But he just sighed.

"He hasn't told you."

"Told me what?"

He turned to her. "He's leaving, Rose. In two weeks. Just like I said."

"Well, yeah," Rose said, "that was the original plan, before . . . everything. But even if he has another job lined up, we can still see each other. It's not hard to fly to another state."

"What about another country?"

The words took her by surprise. "What do you mean?"

"He's going to Europe, Rose. I saw the plane ticket in his room."

"You don't know what you're talking about." She narrowed her eyes at him. "Have you been *snooping in Bodhi's room*?"

"You're not listening. I saw the ticket. In his name. He's leaving. Flying out of JFK on the twenty-eighth."

Fear bloomed quick and full inside her. It was hard even to breathe around it. She stood, her hands shaking as she hurried to untie Coco. She didn't want to hear this. Will was lying. He was jealous, that's all, and he was lying.

"Rose . . ."

"Stop it." She turned on him, standing on the bank of the pond now. "Just stop it, Will."

"I'm trying to help you," he said. "Trying to protect you."

"Yeah, right." She stepped into Coco's saddle and directed her away from the pond.

"It's true," he called after her as she pushed Coco up the hill. "Just ask him, Rose."

Fifty

Bodhi wiped the sweat from his brow as he stepped into the barn. They'd had a couple of brief rain showers since the first big storm, but it wasn't enough to soften the sun-hardened ground. He left the fields each day covered in dust, and he and Rose often went for a swim in the evenings to cool off.

He climbed the ladder, planning to grab a towel and find her. He would take the plane ticket, ask her to go with him to the bank of the pond where they'd shared their first kiss. But when he got to the top, she was already there, sitting on his bed, looking at something in her hands.

He smiled. "Hey! I was just going to look for you."

She didn't look up when he stepped into the loft, and a manic kind of nausea gripped him when he realized that something was wrong.

He lowered himself next to her on the bed and brushed

back a loose strand of her hair. "Hey . . . what's up?"

She didn't answer. Not at first. The sickness inside him grew.

"When were you going to tell me?" she finally said. She turned to look at him. "Or were you going to tell me at all?"

"What do you mean?"

She thrust a piece of paper toward him so that he had no choice but to take it. He didn't have to look to know what it was, but he looked anyway.

His plane ticket to Europe.

"I was going to tell you tonight," he said. "At the pond."

"Tonight?" She stood, pacing the floor. "That's just great. You were going to tell me tonight that you're leaving the country in less than two weeks?"

He took a deep breath. "I'm sorry. I know I should have told you sooner." He ran a hand through his hair. Dust coated his fingers. "I just . . . I didn't know how. And then . . ."

He still didn't know how, and he walked to the plastic bin in the corner and reached under his clean clothes until his hands touched the two pieces of paper he'd stashed there.

He walked over to her and held them out. "It seemed like bad luck to keep your ticket with mine. I thought . . . Well, I wasn't sure if you would come." He hesitated. "I'm still not sure, but I hope you will."

She unfolded the papers, and he saw her eyes travel the length of them before she handed them back to him.

"Looks like you had it all figured out." Her throat rippled as she swallowed, and a moment later, tears started to leak from her eyes. "Get Rose into bed, make her love you, and then spring Europe on her, leave her no choice but to say goodbye."

He shook his head. "Rose . . . what are you saying? None of this was planned. I didn't know I'd fall in love with you. I didn't know I'd never want to be without you again. Everything just . . . happened."

She glared at him through her tears. "We've been together for over a month! You could have told me at any point!"

He nodded, trying to formulate his words, trying to stop the feeling that everything was spinning out of his control toward an end from which he wouldn't be able to return. "You're right. I could have. I should have. But I always planned to ask you to come with me, Rose. Look at the date on that ticket. I bought it the day after that first night we were together."

"And then you told me you would stay!" she shouted. "You told me you would stay *two nights ago*!"

"I meant . . . I meant that I would stay with you, Rose."

She looked at the paper in his hands. "That doesn't look like staying."

He sighed. "I guess I mean that I wanted you to stay with me. That I wanted you to come to Europe. I thought you'd want to come with me."

She crossed her arms over her chest. "There's a big difference between you staying and me going."

He shook his head. "We can't stay here, Rose. It'll kill us both, and I think deep down you know that."

"How do you know what I can and can't do?" she practically shouted at him. "Do you think because we slept together you know everything about me? Is that it?"

He felt like he'd been slapped. "That's not it. I just thought . . . with your mom and everything . . . I guess I thought you might want a fresh start as much as me."

"I can't be with someone who lies to me." A sob broke free from her throat. "How can I ever trust you again? How can I know you're telling me the whole truth?"

She wiped the tears from her face and headed for the ladder.

"Why don't you just admit that you're scared?" he said.

She stopped at the edge of the loft. "Scared? Of what?"

"Of everything!" he said. "Of not having an excuse to stay on the farm anymore! Of leaving your dad and the place where you most remember your mom! Of being forced to live again instead of hiding behind your grief!"

She flushed, and he could see that her hands were shaking as she reached for the ladder. "How . . . how dare you? You don't know me, Bodhi Lowell. You don't know what you're talking about." She started down the ladder.

"Keep telling yourself that, Rose. It's a lot easier than facing the truth."

But she had already disappeared into the barn below, and a moment later, he heard her footsteps loud and fast as she ran from the barn. He stood there, breathing heavy and feeling like someone had punched him in the gut. Then he balled up the printed boarding pass in his hand and threw it across the room.

Fifty-One

Rose lay in bed, the pillow wet under her cheek. She looked at her phone. Eight a.m.

She'd been replaying her conversation with Bodhi all night, alternating between anger and hurt. It didn't matter what he said. He had lied, had led her to believe he would be with her, that they would still be together no matter what. And while he hadn't said they couldn't be together if he went to Europe and she stayed in Milford, the fact that he had bought one-way tickets said it all.

He didn't plan on coming back anytime soon.

And what was all that about her being scared? That's the part that made her the maddest. She wanted to leave the farm, had wanted to travel since she was a kid, and she had the money and box of brochures to prove it. He was just trying to justify what he'd done. He wasn't who she thought he was. Worst of all, Will had been right along.

The barn door slammed shut outside, and she got up and went to the window, wondering what Bodhi was doing. She hadn't helped him with the herd this morning, and she'd spent the hours before sunrise listening to the sound of him moving the cattle out to pasture and settling Mason back into the barn.

Now he bent to pick up his pack, his gaze shifting to the house. She moved back from the window a little, her eyes still on him. He stood there for a minute, backpack in hand, hesitating. Then he started walking, making his way past the house and down the driveway. Something primal and desperate screamed inside her, telling her to go after him, to tell him she loved him and they would work it out. But there was something else, too. A feeling even more powerful than her desire to be with Bodhi, one she couldn't name.

She watched him until he reached the end of the road. When she was sure he couldn't see her leave the house, she bounded down the stairs and headed for the barn.

It felt empty, and it had nothing to do with the fact that the animals had been put out to pasture. It was the absence of something beloved, the void left when the sun went behind a cloud, casting the previously bright world into dark and ominous shadow.

She clambered up the ladder with her heart in her throat, but she wasn't at all surprised to find that everything was gone. Well, not everything. The mattress was gone, probably put back in the bunk room. But all his clothes were missing, the plastic bin empty in the corner. There was a folded piece of paper on the little table he'd gotten from Maggie's consignment shop. Rose's name was written carefully across the front, and for a moment, she thought she might die from the hurt of imagining him sitting at the desk, writing out her name as he prepared to leave her.

She sat down in the rickety wooden chair and opened the letter.

My sweet Rose,

I know you're mad, and I don't blame you. By not telling you my plans, I did lie, even if it was what some people call a lie of omission. That's on me, and I'll always be sorry for it.

When I first saw you that day in the Tractor Supply, I felt like I knew you. You were so familiar to me, right from the beginning. Did I ever tell you that? Then you started talking, and I knew you were special. I saw your strength in the way you looked at me. I heard it in the way you weren't afraid to disagree (even if you were wrong about that nipple for Buttercup).

Then when I got to know you, I realized I didn't know the half of it. You're the strongest person I know. I've never had anything or anyone. Sometimes I think it's true what they say: you can't miss something you never had. But you've had love in your life, real love, and family. I can't even imagine how much it must hurt to have that taken away. You carry that loss with so much grace. I learned every day by watching you. I should have told you that sooner.

I know you care about the farm. It's in your blood, and I can see why. There's so much love there, sometimes I think there's even enough for me. But Rose . . . you deserve a fresh start, too. When you smile and laugh, well, I feel like the whole sky opens up, like the sun is closer to the earth than it's ever been. You don't do it often enough, even now, and I couldn't help wondering if maybe it's because the ghosts of the past are a little too close. Maybe too close to really start over here.

I shouldn't have said what I said though, about you being afraid. Most of the time when I look at you, I don't think you've ever been afraid a day in your life. I'm the one who's afraid, and that's the truth. I'm afraid of never seeing you again, of never feeing the way I do when I'm with you. Most of all I'm afraid that no one will ever look at me like you do. Like I'm not damaged or broken or missing some important part. Like I'm enough. You have that gift, Rose. You make everyone feel so loved. I hope you know it.

Anyway, I'm rambling now. I'm sorry. Nothing makes sense without you. I'm still trying to figure out how I'll live my whole life without you in it. I hope I don't have to.

Here's your plane ticket. You told me you had a passport, that you've had one since you were sixteen. I have some money saved. Not a lot, but enough to get us started. I don't have much of a plan, but I'm thinking that might be what I need. Maybe it's what you need, too, but I trust that you know that better than anyone.

I'll be at Maggie's until I leave next week. Thought that

*might be best. I'll still come by in the mornings and evenings
to take care of the herd, and I'll finish putting up the last of
the hay tomorrow. If you want to talk, you know where to
find me.*

*I'm not leaving you. I know that's what you think, and
I guess I can understand why. But really I'm waiting, Rose.
Waiting for you to say you'll come with me. I'll be waiting
right up until the time I step on that plane. I hope I'll see you
there.*

*I love you, Rose Darrow. I've never loved anyone like I
love you. Whatever happens, I'll carry that love with me for
the rest of my life.*

Bodhi

She looked at the pieces of paper behind the letter. Her
boarding pass and receipt for the ticket. Her heart squeezed
painfully as she refolded the papers. He already felt so far
away. How would she go without him for even one day?
How would she go without him forever?

She folded the letter and ticket and put it in the back
pocket of her shorts. He hadn't left her a choice. Did he really
think she could leave her father? It had been less than a year
since her mother had died. Her dad needed her. The farm
and the animals needed her.

Anger dulled her pain as she made her way back down
the ladder. Bodhi didn't understand. He didn't know what
it was like to have people who counted on you. To carry the
weight of a responsibility like the farm. He passed through

people's lives. He didn't have to stick around when things got tough.

She ignored the voice in her head that called her a liar, that told her Bodhi had been right: she was just scared, plain and simple.

Nothing Bodhi had said in his letter made a difference. Nothing had changed. She would make breakfast for her dad, get back to work on the farm, keep moving forward. It was all there was left to do.

Fifty-Two

"Please tell me I'm not going to have to come up there and drag your butt to Maggie Ryland's house."

Lexie's voice sounded just like it always had. She'd played the part of supportive best friend during Rose's initial phone calls, but in the week since Bodhi had moved to Maggie's house, Lexie had switched tactics, harassing Rose to pack her bags and get out of Milford while she could.

"We've been over this, Lex. I'm not going. I *can't* go," Rose said into the phone.

She was leaning on the fence, watching Buttercup play with some of the other calves while their mothers looked on.

"Can't or won't."

"Can't," Rose said automatically. And then, when she decided to be honest, "Won't. Both, I guess."

"Now we're getting somewhere," Lexie said.

"Don't you have something better to do?" Rose asked. "Like hail a cab or order fancy food or run into your future husband, who will inevitably be a Wall Street trader with a fast car and a good heart?"

"Are you pulling from *Pretty Woman* right now?" Lexie asked.

"Inspired by," Rose said.

"Very funny," Lexie said. "Why are you just getting funny now that I'm not there anymore?"

"It's probably not a coincidence," Rose said.

"I'm not even going to try and analyze that right now, because I know what you're doing."

"What am I doing?" Rose let her gaze travel the field. If she squinted, she could almost believe she saw Bodhi riding Mason in the distance. She had made a point of avoiding him when he came by to take care of the animals every morning and every evening. It hurt to have him close and not talk to him, not feel his arms around her, but it would hurt more to see him and know nothing had changed.

"Trying to distract me. But it won't work." She sighed. "There is no reason why you can't go to Europe. Your dad will figure things out. He's an adult. You've held things together long enough."

"He's not ready." Even as Rose said it, she wasn't so sure. It was true that her dad still wasn't helping much on the farm, but he'd started eating dinner with her at the kitchen table, and now when she found him reading or watching TV, he was usually in the living room instead of the bedroom he had shared with Rose's mother. One time she'd even found him working on the tractor. Actually working on it instead of just sitting on it.

"He'll never be ready if you keep doing everything for him," Lexie said. "And Bodhi leaves tomorrow, so it's kind of now or never, you know?"

"Yeah . . ." Gravel crunched behind her, and she turned around to see Marty's car pulling up in front of the house. "I have to go, Lex. Marty's here."

"Are you just trying to get me off the phone?"

"No, she's really here. I'll talk to you later."

Lexie sighed. "Only if you're calling from the airport."

"Bye, Lex."

Rose hung up and watched as Marty approached. She smiled at Rose, then let her gaze slide to the animals in the field.

"The little one's doing better," she said. "Buttercup, is it?"

Rose nodded. "She's even nursing a little."

Marty laughed. "Just in time to be weaned."

"Right?"

"What finally did the trick?" Marty asked.

"I don't know," Rose said. "It's like she came so close to dying that she finally decided to live."

They were leaning on the fence, making a show of watching the animals, but Rose knew Marty had something to say, could feel it in the weight of the silence.

"Took Bodhi's final check to Maggie's just now," she said. "Wanted to say goodbye."

"That's good," Rose said. But it wasn't good. The thought of saying goodbye to Bodhi made her feel like someone had ripped out her heart.

"Might be good for you, too," Marty said. "At the very least, it's never a good idea to part ways with someone until you've cleared the air."

"Did you clear the air with Tseng?" Rose asked.

Marty sucked in a deep breath, like the question hurt her to consider.

"I'm sorry," Rose said. "That was mean. I just . . . I don't know how to handle this."

Marty reached over and smoothed her hair. "I wish I could say it gets easier."

Rose looked at her. "It doesn't?"

Marty gave her a lopsided grin. "Just more familiar."

"Great."

"Then again," Marty said, "maybe you'll be smarter than me."

"What do you mean?"

Marty sighed. "I don't know, Rose. . . . Sometimes I feel like I've been running my whole life."

"Running from what?"

Marty shrugged. "Feelings. Love. Complication. Mom and Dad loved the farm and each other so much. They were happy here, I guess, but it just seemed to me like they were trapped. I never wanted love if that's what it meant."

"It doesn't have to, does it?" Rose asked.

Marty looked at her. "What would it mean if it doesn't mean that?"

Rose thought about it. "Being really free. Being yourself with someone and doing all the things you want to do, but doing them together." She looked into her aunt's eyes, and for the first time she saw a woman. Not Marty or her aunt, but a woman who felt fear and happiness, who had loved and lost. "Can't you have love your way?"

"Can't you?" Marty asked.

Rose shook her head. "It's different with me and Bodhi. He's going to Europe."

"I know," she said. "He told me. But he wants you to go with him. Wouldn't that be love your way?"

"No, it wouldn't. I can't just run off to Europe with a guy. I have Dad and the farm to think about."

"First of all, something tells me Bodhi is more than just a guy," Marty said. "And second, you're not sixty, Rose. You're barely eighteen. You don't have to think about anyone but yourself." Rose started to interrupt, to tell Marty she was wrong, when Marty stopped her. "I understand why you stepped up after your mother died. Your dad was in a bad place. He needed time to figure out what his life was going to look like without her. In a perfect world, he would have been able to take care of you while you figured that out, too, but it didn't work out that way. He was lucky to have you. But it's time. It's time for all of us to move on."

Tears sprang to Rose's eyes. "I don't want to move on. I want to remember what she looked like when she rode the tractor with Dad or when she made daisy chains out of wildflowers or when she stood on the porch in her apron."

"Oh, Rose . . ." Marty reached out, touched her hair. "Is

that what you think? That leaving will make you forget?" Marty's smile was sad. "If only it were that easy."

"This is where I feel her most," Rose said softly.

"I understand that," Marty said. "But you haven't been anywhere else. How do you know you won't feel her standing on a bridge over the Danube? Or watching the sun set from the Eiffel Tower? Or looking out at the sea in Scotland?"

"She never went to those places."

"No," Marty said, "but she wanted you to go there. And you know what?"

"What?"

"I think she'll be with you every step of the way, wherever you are. She wouldn't want you to stay here nursing your grief when you could be out in the world finding joy. And there's something else you might not realize about your mom."

"What's that?" Rose asked.

"She was no coward. Love was everything to her. She would have risked everything for it, and I think if she were here, she'd tell you to do the same."

Rose turned back to the animals. "It's probably too late anyway. I don't even have a backpack."

Marty laughed. "Now you're getting desperate." She put an arm around Rose and squeezed. "I'm not your mom. This is all the pep talk I've got. But I hope you'll think about it, because this life is a lot shorter than it seems."

Fifty-Three

"I think that's it." Bodhi set his pack on the floor of Maggie Ryland's kitchen and sat down at the table where she was having coffee, the sky barely lightening outside the window. He'd said goodbye to Marty the day before when she dropped off his check. Now there was nothing to do but go to the airport and accept that Rose wasn't coming.

"Well, damn it," Maggie said. "I'm going to miss you."

He smiled. "I'll miss you, too. Thanks for . . . Well, for everything."

"I should be thanking you. I don't think I realized how bored I was until I started sticking my nose in yours and Rose's business."

He laughed, but it only lasted a second. "Not that it did any good."

She sighed, reaching across the table to put her hand on

his. "This life is a lot longer than people think."

"Then why do people say 'life is short'?"

"Because they forget all the chances they've had to make things right," she said. "Leave me your email address. I'll pass it to Rose if she changes her mind. Who knows? Maybe one day you'll be standing in front of Notre Dame, and you'll look up, and there she'll be."

He smiled. "You're being romantic."

"Maybe," she said. "But life is romantic if you look at it like that, and I always have."

"Will she be okay here?" he asked her.

"The Darrows come from tough stock. She'll be okay, but that doesn't mean she'll be happy."

"I want her to be happy," he said.

Maggie shook her head. "That's not up to you. None of us can do that work for someone else. I'm afraid we're the president and CEO when it comes to our own happiness. The buck stops with us."

"I guess you're right." He stood, wiping his hands on his jeans. "I guess I better be heading out. The bus leaves in less than an hour."

She got up from the table. "I wish you'd let me take you to the airport."

He smiled. "I'm considering it the first leg of my journey."

"Good for you." She stepped toward him, and he wrapped his arms around her in a hug. "Make yourself happy," she said quietly. "You deserve it, son, and don't let anyone ever tell you different."

He nodded, then turned away so she wouldn't see the tears in his eyes. "See you, Maggie."

He picked up his pack and left before he could get even more sentimental. He chided himself. Milford had changed him. Turned him soft. But he knew it was a lie as soon as he thought it. It wasn't Milford that had changed him but a green-eyed girl with fiery hair and a spine of steel. He wouldn't forget her.

He turned onto the sidewalk in front of Maggie's house and headed for the bus station on Main Street.

Fifty-Four

Rose woke up suddenly, her eyes adjusting to the blue light of a cloudy morning. She'd heard something outside, and she searched her mind for it, trying to pull the sound out of the haze of sleep.

A car door. That was it.

She got up and walked to the window just in time to see the taillights of Marty's car disappearing down the drive. She looked at her phone. 8:02 a.m.

Marty didn't usually get out of bed until at least nine, and Rose stood there in the dim morning light, trying to figure out what would prompt her aunt to make such an early visit.

A few seconds later, she thought she heard the clink of dishes in the kitchen, and she walked across the room to her bedroom door and listened, wondering if she was imagining it. But no, there it was again. Someone was definitely down there.

She'd planned to sleep in. After today, she'd be back on the four a.m. shift, herding the animals by herself in the dark. She tried not to think about it. The idea of riding without Bodhi, of doing everything without him, was still an open wound somewhere in the vicinity of her heart.

But she was awake now, and she made her way down the stairs and into the kitchen where she found her dad sitting at the table with a steaming mug in front of him.

"Dad?"

He looked up. "Hi, honey. Did I wake you?"

She sat in the chair across from him. "No. I heard Marty's car outside."

He took a drink of his coffee, then nodded. "Just left."

"What was she doing here so early?" Rose asked. "Did she have something to tell Bodhi before he left?"

"Bodhi wasn't here this morning," he said.

"Then who . . . The animals . . ."

"I took care of the herd this morning," he said.

It took her a minute to process the information. "Is everything okay, Dad?"

He looked down at the mug. "Everything hasn't been okay for a long time," he finally said. "But I guess you know that better than anyone."

"What do you mean?"

Her met her eyes, and she was surprised to realize he was looking at her, really looking at her, for the first time in a long time. "Having Bodhi here . . . Well, it just gave me an excuse to keep doing what I was doing." Rose flinched at the sound of Bodhi's name, said casually, like he could have been anybody. Her dad continued. "But it wasn't right, and it especially wasn't right to make you think you had to stay."

"Dad . . ."

He held up a hand to stop her. "Let me say what I have to say, Rose."

She nodded.

"I know you love the farm," he said. "But loving something—or someone—should free you, not make you a prisoner. You didn't apply to college because your mom was sick. I understand that. But she's gone, Rose." He met her eyes. "She's really gone. And we're still here, so we have to figure out how to be happy without her."

She was surprised to feel the moisture of tears on her cheeks. She swiped at them with one hand. "It sucks."

He nodded. "It sure does. But it's what your mom would want. The farm will always be here for you. But Bodhi . . . Well, there's no guarantee there. Your mom was a sucker for love, and if she were here, she'd be throwing your suitcase into the car and dragging you to the airport with your hands tied if she had to."

"What about the farm?"

"What about it?" He smiled. "Been running this farm since your mom and I took it over twenty years ago. I imagine I can still handle it."

She looked down at her hands. "I don't even know if he still wants me to go."

"If he has an ounce of sense in his head—and I have a

feeling he does—he'll never stop loving you, honey."

"I'm not packed . . . I don't have a backpack or . . . anything."

"Sounds like you're looking for excuses, Rose." He reached across the table and put his big hand over her smaller one. "And the Darrows don't make excuses when there's something to be done, now do we?"

"I guess not."

"I imagine if you get moving now, you can still make that flight," he said.

There was a sudden lightening inside her, like the moment they throw off the ropes on a hot air balloon, the moment you rise into the sky and realize you've been seeing the world through a pinhole instead of a picture window.

She walked around to her father's side of the table. "Thank you, Daddy."

She headed for the hallway before she could talk herself out of it.

"Rose?" her dad said as she reached the door.

"Yeah?"

"Marty left something for you in the foyer that might help with your packing problem."

She hurried down the hall. Something was leaning against the door, a hulking mass in the early morning shadows. It was only when she got closer that she realized it was a giant backpack. She recognized it from the last time she and her mother had picked Marty up at the airport.

It was Marty's old pack.

A piece of paper was pinned to the top. Rose leaned down, reading her aunt's sloppy handwriting.

Time to go. See you on the other side of the world. xxoo

For a few seconds she was frozen in place. Then she grabbed the backpack and ran for the stairs.

Fifty-Five

The shuttle got Bodhi to the airport a full six hours before his flight, but it was the only bus from Milford that day, and there was no way he was going to mention the timetable to Maggie. She would have insisted on driving him to the airport, and he didn't want her to go to the trouble. She'd done enough for him.

He got off the bus and stepped under the awning outside the terminal. After an almost entirely dry summer, the sky had opened up. It had been pouring buckets since Bodhi had left Maggie's that morning.

He took one last look at the New York sky, the clouds thick and ominous overhead, blocking out almost all the light from the sun. He would miss the soft air on the farm, the shuffle of the animals under the hayloft, the way the sun set orange and lilac behind the mountains. Most of all he would miss Rose, the gentle strength of her hand in his and the way her smile lit up all the places inside him that had been dark for so long.

But she wasn't coming, and by this time tomorrow there would be thousands of miles between them. He felt hollowed out thinking about it, but he couldn't change it, so he would have to find a way to get used to it.

He shifted his pack on his back, getting used to the weight all over again, and walked through the sliding doors.

Fifty-Six

Rose dragged the pack down the hall, wondering how she'd ever haul it through Europe on her back. She'd find a way, and it wouldn't matter, because she would be with Bodhi. That was all that mattered. She saw that now.

Her dad was waiting at the bottom of the stairs when she got there. "You sure you won't let me drive you?"

"I think I need the time to figure out what I'm going to say when I get there," she said.

He nodded. "Let me know where you park the truck and I'll have Maggie take me down to pick it up." He reached for the pack. "I'll get this outside for you."

"It's okay," she said. "I have to get used to carrying it anyway."

His eyes were sad, but he smiled anyway. "You have your passport?"

"Yep. And my driver's license."

"Money?" he asked.

"I've been saving for three years. I have enough, I think."

"Call me if you run short." He handed her a Windbreaker from the hook by the door. "You're going to need this."

She slipped it on.

"And call or email along the way so I know you're okay," he said.

She laughed. "Don't worry. I'll be fine."

He held open his arms, and she stepped into them, hugging him with more force than she intended. They stood like that for a long moment.

"I love you, honey, and wherever your mom is, she's cheering for you right now. Look for her if you need her. I think you'll find that she's right there."

She nodded, choking on a sob. "She's right there when you need her, too, Dad. And so am I."

He hugged her fiercely and kissed her forehead. "Better go. You've got a plane to catch."

She stepped away from him and knew for sure Bodhi had been right. She'd been scared. Scared to say goodbye to her dad and the farm. And, yes, scared to lose sight of her mom, too. But now she didn't want to be afraid. She wanted to be free.

"I love you, Daddy."

She grabbed the backpack and half carried, half dragged it to the truck, the rain beating on the hood of the Windbreaker like noisy little pellets.

She'd thrown the pack in the passenger side of the truck and was opening the driver's side door when she caught sight of Will making his way up the driveway in the rain. She watched as he approached, wondering if he would turn and make for the house, but he kept walking until he was right in front of her.

"Hey," he said.

"Hey."

"So you're going."

"How did you know?" she asked.

"Your dad was at my place today, talking to my dad about hiring some extra help, I think."

Rose nodded.

He took a deep breath. "I'm sorry, Rose. For everything."

She smiled. "It's okay."

"It's not. You're the best friend I've ever had. You've always wanted what's best for me, and you've always wanted me to be happy."

"Well, if it makes you feel any better, you were right about Bodhi leaving," she said. "I mean, I understand why he didn't tell me, but you were looking out for me. I can't be mad about that."

He met her eyes. "But I wasn't doing it for you, Rose. I was doing it for me. Because I wanted to keep you here, even if that meant you were unhappy." His breath came out in a shudder. "I guess I have a lot to learn about love."

She leaned forward and wrapped her arms around his waist, resting her head on his chest. "Don't we all."

"I'll miss you," he said into the top of her head.

She looked up at him. "I'll miss you, too. But I'll be back, and you can always shoot me an email if you want to meet up on the road."

His gaze scanned the fields, wet with rain, fog laying low in patches. "I don't think so. This is where I belong."

"You know what's really amazing?" she asked.

"What?"

"It's never too late to change your mind. And if you don't, I'll still be here if you need me."

He smiled. "I'm counting on it." He opened the door of the truck. "Better get a move on. Traffic's going to be a nightmare."

She got into the truck and looked back at him. "I love you, Will."

He smiled. "I love you, too."

She turned the key in the ignition and put the car in gear. She had almost reached the end of the driveway when she caught sight of Buttercup frolicking in the rain with a couple of the other calves. But that wasn't what got her attention. It was the tag missing from Buttercup's ear.

Maybe Buttercup would be waiting when she got back, too.

She took her foot off the brake and continued to the end of the driveway. She only dared one glance in the rearview mirror. She saw it all. Will, standing in the rain with his hands in his pockets. The farm. Her father. Maybe even the shimmer of her mother on the porch. But they lived in her, too. She would carry them with her.

And she would live. She would live.

Fifty-Seven

Two and a half hours later, she was creeping forward in bumper-to-bumper traffic, still five miles from the airport. The rain that had eluded them all summer now seemed like a waterfall overhead. The taillights in front of her were nothing but red smudges through the torrent, and she leaned forward in the seat, her gaze moving between the cars and the time on her phone.

The plane Bodhi had booked them on was due to leave in a couple of hours. She thought she'd heard somewhere that you had to check in at least an hour in advance. What if she got there too late?

She couldn't think about that. It was too awful to imagine. She would get there. She had to.

Fifty-Eight

"We will now begin boarding for flight 9672 to Edinburgh. You may begin preboarding if you have small children or require special assistance."

Bodhi listened to the announcement with a mixture of relief and dread. He'd spent the last five hours in the airport, replaying every moment between him and Rose, starting with the first time he'd seen her. It seemed like a lifetime ago, but also somehow close enough to touch. Like it might be within his power to step into another dimension, one where he hadn't made such a mess of things, where he'd told Rose the truth from the beginning. If he could, she might be here with him right now, and it suddenly felt like everything was out of balance, like the earth itself was wobbling on its axis.

He dared a glance at the long tile walkway, then chided himself for doing it. *Stupid.*

"Attention passengers for flight 9672 from New York to Edinburgh; we will now begin boarding Groups A through C."

He stood and picked up his pack.

Fifty-Nine

Rose parked the truck and put the keys in the glove box. Then she dragged Marty's pack—her pack now—out of the backseat. Getting it on wasn't easy, but the plane left in a little over an hour. She would have to run to make it, and she couldn't run dragging the pack behind her.

Heaving it onto her shoulders, she snapped the strap at her waist and took off for the terminal as fast as the giant backpack would allow.

A TSA employee pointed her to customs, and by the time she got into line at security, her heart was pounding against the inside of her chest, and not just because she'd been running. Bodhi was here. In this airport. If she could just get through security in time, she would never make the mistake of walking away from him again.

She bounced up and down a little, like that would somehow get her there faster, as she wound her way closer to the agent checking IDs and boarding passes. When she finally reached the head of the line, she thrust her paperwork at a bored-looking guy in his twenties with thin shoulders and a military haircut.

He looked up at her. "This plane is already boarding."

"I figured," she said, looking around him at the line in front of the x-ray machines.

He blinked at her. "We're not supposed to let you through if it's boarding."

"I understand," she said, "but this is an emergency."

He raised an eyebrow. "An emergency?"

"Well, not like a medical emergency or anything, but a . . . a life emergency?" He didn't say anything, so she kept going. "Please . . . if you don't let me through, the love of my life is going to get on a plane without me, and he's going to think I don't want to go with him. But I do. I really, really do. And if I don't, if I get stuck here and he leaves, everything will stay the same. I won't get to see if my mother is still with me in Paris or Hungary, and I'll never know if the life I have is the one I chose or just the one I settled for."

She was breathing fast when she was through. She wondered if the man would make her turn around, or worse, have her taken into custody for a psych evaluation. Instead he sighed, and she thought she saw something like understanding in his eyes.

He circled the gate number on her boarding pass. "Better hurry. We don't want everything to stay the same, now do we?"

She grinned. "No, sir. Thank you!"

She rushed forward, took off her shoes, and threw the pack on the belt. Less than two minutes later, she was running down the carpeted hall to the gate on her boarding pass.

She raced past passengers with suitcases and a few with backpacks like hers, past Starbucks and Waterstones, past security guards and flight attendants. People stopped to stare, some of them smiling, some of them annoyed when she accidentally jostled them.

Then the gate was there, ominously empty, up ahead. She didn't stop running until she reached it, but by then, an airline employee in a blue suit was closing the door to the ramp that led to the plane.

"Wait!" She stopped, panting. "Wait. That's my . . . that's my plane."

"Sorry. The captain has already secured the cabin door."

Panic spread like a wildfire inside her. Bodhi was on that plane, and he was leaving without her, without even knowing how much she loved him. "Please . . . I have to get on that plane."

"It's against FAA regulations," he said, locking the door. "We can't open it now."

She stepped backward, dropping her pack on one of the chairs. She was too late. It was over, and she almost doubled over with the unfairness of it. She had finally chosen to live, and the person who had made her want to do it was gone.

"Rose?"

The voice came from far away, familiar but impossible.

Still she turned toward it, and he was there, right in front of her. He pulled his backpack off his shoulder and let it drop to the ground.

"Bodhi . . ." She looked back at the locked door, the plane visible through the window, pulling away from the gate. "Your plane . . ."

He stepped toward her. "Our plane. It was supposed to be our plane."

"But why aren't you on it?" she asked.

He shrugged. "Decided a new beginning was more dependent on company than location." He sighed. "I just want to be with you, Rose. I don't care where we are."

"Me too." She took a deep breath. "I'm sorry. I . . . You were right. I was scared, and I used you as an excuse instead of admitting it."

"And now?"

She saw the caution in his eyes, a scar from all the times he'd been hurt and let down before. She took a step closer to him. "The truth?"

"Always."

"I'm still scared." She laughed a little. "Terrified actually."

"Would it help if I said I was scared, too?" he asked, sliding his arms around her shoulders.

"A little," she admitted.

"I'm scared, too," he said. "But nothing could ever scare me as much as living without you."

She nodded. "So we're in it together then."

"I think so."

"What about our plane?"

He bent his head until their lips were only inches apart. "We'll catch the next one."

She smiled, and when she closed her eyes she could see them all, everyone who was scared and sad and lost but living anyway. She saw Marty on the back of a motorcycle, clutching Tseng's waist, weaving through a market full of exotic fruit and strange languages. She saw Maggie Ryland, missing her dead husband but cooking for neighbors and daring to open her heart to people like Rose and Bodhi and Rose's father. She saw her dad, too, starting again, riding Mason as the sun came up, orange and pink and gold.

They were all scared sometimes, but they were brave. They were living.

Bodhi slipped his arms around her waist and pulled her to him. Then his mouth was on hers, and she knew that it would be okay. She and Bodhi would be brave, too. They would live.

And they would do it together.

Acknowledgments

Thanks again go to Steven Malk for continuing to have informed my career in the best way possible. I feel so lucky to be his client, and just as lucky to have on my side the passion and wisdom of everyone at Writers House. It's true what they say: no agent is better than a bad agent. But let me tell you; a great agent is worth his weight in gold, and I am lucky enough to have worked with one for the past eight years.

Thank you to Jennifer Klonsky, for making this process so collaborative, for contributing your special brand of wit and wisdom, and most of all for being willing to invest in me and my work. Getting to be one of your authors is a high point in my career. I hope we get to do lots more books together!

Thanks also to HarperCollins Publishers and everyone

at HarperTeen who has given my work a home. This is especially true for publicist Stephanie Hoover, who goes above and beyond to get the word out, and associate editor Catherine Wallace, who sees to a million and one important things behind the scenes. Thanks also to Alison Klapthor, Alison Donalty, and Sarah Kaufman for keeping it fresh with this lovely cover even when it meant going back to the drawing board, and to copy editor Beth Potter for seeing to the little things I'm sometimes too distracted to see.

Thank you to Allison and Rich Blazeski, who so generously shared their farm and memories of their beautiful son, Alex. It is extraordinary to open your hearts to those around you when suffering such a terrible loss. Allison and Rich have done this in spades, both with me personally and with our community. Because of them, Alex lives on in our hearts, and I hope in some small way I've managed to capture his unique love for farming and the very best parts of small-town life. Alex and the whole Blazeski family are certainly one of them. Any technical errors are my own.

Thank you to dear friends M. J. Rose, Jenny Draeger, Anne Rought, Tonya Hurley, Jenny Milchman, and everyone who makes the writing community warm, welcoming, and inspiring. Thanks also to those of you who are such loyal readers and staunch supporters online. You have all seen me through a dark day somewhere along the way.

To my mother, Claudia Baker, and my father, Michael St. James: finally . . . FINALLY I wouldn't want to be anyone but me. Thank you.

And to Kenneth, Rebekah, Andrew, and Caroline, for showing me how to be brave, and most of all, how to live. You have my thanks, and my heart.

Read on for a peek at Michelle Zink's *Lies I Told*

Prologue

Looking back, I should have known Playa Hermosa was the beginning of the end. We'd had a good run, and if things were sometimes tense between Mom, Dad, and Parker, it was nothing a new job couldn't fix. Just when they'd be at each other's throats, we'd move on to another town.

And there was nothing like a new town to remind us which team we were on.

But Playa Hermosa was different. It was like another world. One where the old rules didn't apply. Like the exotic birds on the peninsula, we were suddenly all on our own.

Except it didn't feel like that right away. In the beginning, it was business as usual. Plot the con, get into character, work our way in, stick together.

I don't know if it was my relationship with Logan that tipped everything over the edge or if the signs had been there long before. Either way, I tell myself it was for the best. The universe seems to have its own mysterious plan. I guess we're just along for the ride. I can live with that. The harder part, the impossible part, is living with what I did to Logan and his family.

We knew what we were doing. Knew the risks. But Logan and his family were *good*. Maybe the first really good people I'd ever met. They loved one another, sacrificed for one another. Not because they didn't have anyone else, but because that's what love is.

What happened to them is my fault. And I'm still trying to figure out how to live with that.

Then there's Parker. Deep down, I know the choice was his. But I can't help wondering if he stuck around because of me. If he hadn't, everything would be different, and he'd probably be drinking beer in Barcelona or coffee in Paris or something.

I can't think about the other stuff. Thinking about it forces me back to the question: Why didn't I see it? Had the end of our family been one sudden, impulsive decision setting into motion a string of events that changed everything? Or had it all been a long time coming? I think that would be worse, because if it was true, it meant that I was hopelessly, unforgivably naive.

And there's no crime as unforgivable as naivety when you're on the grift.

One

I swam my way up from sleep, trying to remember where I was against a mechanical roar outside the window. The room didn't help. Filled with the standard furniture and a few unpacked boxes, it could have been any bedroom in any house in any city in America.

I ran down the list of possibilities: Chicago, New York, Maryland, and then Phoenix, because that was where we'd worked last. But it only took a few seconds to realize that none of them were right. We'd arrived the day before in Playa Hermosa, a peninsula that jutted out over the Pacific Ocean somewhere between Los Angeles and San Diego.

It was like a different world, the slickness of Los Angeles falling away as we entered an almost tropical paradise, shady with low-hanging trees and dominated by Spanish architecture. I caught glimpses of the Pacific, a sheet of shimmering blue silk in the distance, as my dad navigated the Audi up the winding roads and my mom pointed things out along the way. Parker sat silently beside me in the backseat, brooding and sullen like he always was when we started a new job. We'd passed fields, overgrown with dry brush, that led to turnouts where people could stop and take pictures. We didn't take any, because that was one of the most important rules: leave no proof.

And there were more rules where that one came from, rules that allowed us to run cons in affluent communities all over the country, worming our way into the lives of wealthy neighbors and trust-fund babies with more money than sense. Rules that allowed us to make off with tens of thousands of dollars, staying in place just long enough after every theft to insure that we weren't under the cloud of suspicion. That was one of the worst parts: staying put, pretending to be as shocked and innocent as everyone else.

Only after the dust settled would we move on, citing a job transfer or start-up opportunity for my dad and changing our identification through one of his underground sources. If anyone ever suspected us of committing a crime, we were too long gone to know about it.

A portion of each take was split between us, the rest of it used to set up the next con. From the looks of things, it hadn't been cheap this time around.

The roar of the leaf blower outside grew louder as it moved under the window, and I put my pillow over my head, trying to block out the noise. We'd spent the last few weeks in a hotel in Palm Springs, preparing for the Playa Hermosa job, but I still wasn't ready to face my first day in a new school. There had been too many of them. Right now, in this unfamiliar room, I was in a pleasant kind of limbo, the last town far enough away to be a memory, the new one still a figment of my imagination.

But it was no use. The down in my pillow was no match for the rumble outside, and I finally tossed it aside and got out of bed, digging around in a still-packed box until I found a hair tie. My gaze was drawn to the reflection in the mirror over the dresser. The brown hair was a surprise. I hadn't been a brunette since Seattle, and I still approached every mirror half expecting to see my face framed by a sheet of straight, shiny blond hair. My eyes—a dark blue—were the only thing I could count on to be the same when we moved from city to city. But they were a little different now, too. Older, shadowed with something weary that echoed the way I'd felt ever since our near miss in Maryland the year before.

Lately, it had begun to feel like too much. Too much lying. Too much risk. Too much *work*. I had been eleven when I was adopted by my mom and dad. I'd spent a year thinking my life would be normal, then Parker joined the family and we were quickly initiated into life on the grift. It had been nonstop ever since. I hadn't been this tired since my fifth foster home, back when survival meant dodging a woman who was a little too quick with the back of her hand, her son a little too generous with the creepy glances.

I leaned away from the mirror and took a deep breath, forcing the past back into the dark corners of my mind where it belonged. Then I reached into the unpacked box, feeling past my books, the little makeup I owned, the one framed photograph I had of our family. When my hand brushed against a smooth wooden container, I pulled it from the box.

It was a simple unfinished rectangle, the kind you could buy in any craft store for five bucks. It was meant to be a jewelry or treasure box, but I'd never gotten around to decorating or staining it. I probably never would. Its contents were against the rules. I'd never be able to keep it out long enough to make it look nice.

Anyway, that wasn't the point. It was the stuff inside that mattered, and I reached for the flimsy gold clasp and lifted the lid, pushing aside the carousel ticket from Chicago, the postcard from DC, the cheap plastic taxicab I'd bought from a street vendor in New York City. Finally, I found what I was looking for, and I brought the plastic ID card—*Chandler High School* emblazoned across the top—close to my face for a better look.

My teeth were white and straight in the picture, my blond hair shining even in the crappy fluorescent lighting. The picture belied none of the fear and anxiety I'd felt in Phoenix. I could have been any popular high school student. A cheerleader. Class president. Lead in the school play.

The ID was dangerous, against the rules. All my mementos were. But they were the only things that made me feel real, that made real all the places I'd been, all the people I'd met. Sometimes I thought my forbidden trinkets were the only proof I existed at all.

I closed the wooden container and placed it back in the still-packed box. Then I slipped the ID card into the pocket of my boxers, pulled my hair into a loose ponytail, and stepped out into the hallway.

Two

The house wasn't huge, but already it was one of my favorites. I ran my hand along the walls as I headed for the stairs, enjoying the rough feel of plaster under my fingertips. The house was authentic in a way the McMansion outside Chicago hadn't been, its walls and windows more solid than in the flimsy house we'd rented in Phoenix. That one had looked fancy on the outside, but the walls were thin, the windows so poorly sealed that a steady stream of hot air blew on my face when I lay in bed during the 115-degree summer.

This one was nice, even if I didn't recognize any of the furniture, which we'd bought brand-new like we did at the start of every new job. At first it had been hard, leaving everything behind at the end of each con. But like a lot of things, I'd gotten used to it. Now I could pack my clothes and books in less than fifteen minutes.

I took the staircase to the main floor, the giant ceiling fan whirring softly in the tall-ceilinged foyer, and headed for the kitchen at the back of the house.

Parker was already there, sitting at a table under a bank of open windows and spooning cereal into his mouth while he read the business section. I hardly thought about my share of the money we earned, but Parker was obsessive, determined to invest his piece of each take so he wouldn't have to rely on Cormac and Renee—or anyone like them— ever again. Articles and books about stocks, bonds, and IPOs were his reading material of choice, something that stood in contrast to his new appearance. It was always a little weird watching everyone in the family transform, and I stood in the doorway, trying to get used to this new version of my brother.

He'd ditched the preppy young Republican he'd played in Phoenix in favor of a Southern California surfer boy. The longer hair worked on him. Dark blond and a little messy, it made him look like he'd just climbed out of the water. He was my brother in everything but blood, yet I could understand why girls fell all over themselves for his attention. With his perfect white teeth, strong jaw, and boyish dimples, he was every girl's type. Add in the bad-boy brood, and he was basically irresistible.

I glanced at the lines of leather cord marching up his arm, strategically placed to hide his scars. I'd asked him about the bracelets once, wondering why he wore them in any kind of weather, even when long sleeves covered his arms all the way to his wrists. He'd just shrugged and said, "They remind me who I really am."

I didn't understand it. I wanted nothing more than to forget the past, riddled with unfamiliar beds and unfamiliar faces. But Parker didn't want to forget. The past was what drove him, and I had a sudden flash of him at thirteen, the day he'd been adopted into the family, eyes hooded, his forearm wrapped in gauze. In a foster care system that had seen everything, Parker's record had rendered him unplaceable in another home.

Even good-hearted people didn't want to come home to a bathroom covered in blood.

It made my heart hurt to remember Parker that way, alone and unwanted. I shut the memory down and sat across from him at the table.

"Hey," I said quietly, not wanting to startle him.

He looked up, his eyes a little glazed. "Hey."

He lowered his eyes back to the paper, and I looked around the room, surprised by the lack of moving boxes on the counters and floor.

"Wow . . . Mom must have really gone to town unpacking last night."

"You know how she is," Parker said, not looking up.

As if on cue, the sound of heels clicking on tile sounded from the hall. A couple of seconds later my mom walked into the room, trim and lithe in white slacks and a halter top that managed to look both classy and subtly sexy. It was one of her many gifts: the ability to fit into any town in a matter of